I0817789

Old Monsters
Stories Inspired by the Classics

FIRST EDITION
Published December 2025
By Indies United Publishing House, LLC

Cover Art by Cassandra Harris
Edited by Jayne Southern www.bookaholiceditor.com

This book is a work of fiction. References to real people, events, establishments, organizations, or locales are intended only to provide a sense of authenticity, and are used fictitiously. All other names, characters, places and incidents in this publication are fictitious or are used fictitiously, are drawn from the author's imagination and are not to be construed as real. Any resemblances to real persons, living or dead, events or locales is entirely coincidental

Some images in this publication were generated using artificial intelligence tools and may not be subject to copyright protection.

ISBN 978-1-64456-879-8 [Hardcover]
ISBN 78-1-64456-880-4 [Paperback]
ISBN 978-1-64456-881-1 [Kindle]
ISBN 978-1-64456-882-8 [ePub]

Library of Congress Control Number: 2025927408

INDIES UNITED PUBLISHING HOUSE, LLC
P.O. BOX 3071
QUINCY, IL 62305-3071
indiesunited.net

Table of Contents

OLD MONSTERS

D. Krauss

Preface

We are the first generation to sit up Saturday nights and get the bejeezus scared out of us by Frankenstein, the Wolfman, ghosts, and whatever other 1930s-through-1950s monsters, the hosts of those schlocky late-night horror shows—*Vampira, Doctor Shock, Svengooli* ... and the legend, Elvira—could dig up. Every Podunk television station serving a sparse and scattered populace had one of these shows. In Dothan, Alabama, WTVY, it was *X Minus 1*, with the appropriate reverb at the title announcement. There was no host for that show, but a decent intro of movie stills and a segment of *Swan Lake* which, taken out of context, is pretty eerie music.

I still remember, quite clearly, sitting on the couch, hiding under the afghan with my brother and sister, and watching *The Daughter of Dr. Jekyll,* all of us so frightened during the mirror transformation scene that we immediately shut off the TV and hid, trembling, until we fell asleep. And had nightmares.

By today's standards, it's a fairly tame scene, even hokey. Special effects were rubber bats and excessive makeup back then, and didn't fool anybody. But it was the idea that, outside the bedroom window and lurking in the woods, was a monster, something unnatural and murderous that wanted your soul and your life, and you were helpless before it. Whispering, "It's only a movie," over and over, and the ghosts were gone by sunrise, and your mother absolutely forbade you to watch those shows anymore but, yeah, right, Mom. In the safe and normal world sixty years ago, it was thrilling to think that maybe, just maybe, things weren't that safe and normal.

As it turns out.

I am the first to admit that the more recent horror movies are vastly superior to the clunky and laughable ones of those middle decades. The *Nosferatu* remake beats the original into oblivion—which is heresy—but, there it is. The newer ones are more plausible; we have discovered that monsters are somewhat real and take every form you can imagine; some of them looking very much like your next-door neighbor, or a national politician. There is no garlic or silver or incantation that will save you from you. Those old rubber mask monsters have become quaint.

Like radio. Like Sputnik and nuclear attack drills. All nostalgia and amusement now but, in their day, the cutting edge, the frontier between a life of surety and the dark. Those old monsters from the Hammer and RKO films, *Creepy* and *Vampirella* magazines, birthed *The Walking Dead,* and Jason, and *Alien*. And still inspire.

Here, then, are ten tales inspired by the monsters I trembled at through afghan holes on a Saturday night decades ago, and who've chased me ever since.

ASPECTS OF A TRADITIONAL VAMPIRE AND THE NEED TO DISPATCH SAME

Aspects of a Traditional Vampire and the Need to Dispatch Same

(Nov 2013, InfectiveInk Magazine)

Randall lived on a small two-acre lot off the Enterprise Road, in a tiny house built in the 50s and never upgraded. No need; he was alone and spartan. He'd moved there some years ago for the isolation and quiet, which he did need.

Glen lived two miles up the New Brockton Road and down a gravel lane behind a cotton field and was, also, isolated and quiet, except he'd lived this rural Alabama life since birth and had the mournful displeasure of watching his widespread family precede him through various methods, such as the Vietnam War, both Iraq Wars, car accidents, and one to the overzealous ministrations of a particularly drunken Klan attack.

They knew each other by a chance remark Randall made when both happened to be in Wood's Store, the little one-room convenience shop, run by a couple even more ancient than they were; one of the few places an old Black man like Glen could get necessities without harassment. Randall was standing next to the ancient Nehi Grape Soda box located against the bare pine wall, under a faded

Massey Ferguson pin-up calendar. "Knight to Queen's four, checkmate," he'd said when he located a YooHoo pop bottle, since those were rare now.

Glen, peering at some rather dated cans of tuna nearby, looked up in surprise. "You play chess?"

"Used to."

And so Glen and Randall started playing once a week, quickly expanding to three to four times as their camaraderie grew. They played at each other's houses on a random schedule, splitting wins and losses just as randomly, which was the joy of being evenly matched. They spoke nothing of each other's past and tragedies, the books written clearly on their faces, and because that was then and this was now, the dwindling of their lives; and it was a pleasant way to pass what little time was left.

In the way of small towns and passed-by regions, they were tolerated. Two silly old men playing chess, and driving around together in cars too old to bear much more use, seen at the Piggly-Wiggly in Enterprise gathering food and often on each other's porches late at night, a chess board and a bottle of Jack between them. Old White men and old Black men could mix because they were rather harmless together, but there were still peanut-farmer traditions to uphold. "Coupla old queers," Davis, the red-neckiest of all the peanut farmers, spat one day when both of them happened to be at Spencer's, the three-room convenience store (with gas pumps, no less) in the middle of Goodlyn. Glen had given Davis the disgusted look allowed by old Black men at the end of their toleration of redneck culture, but Randall gave him something else. It was a look of disquietude, of promised violence with capability. Davis, made uncomfortable, muttered and walked off, uncertain, and the witnessing rednecks shied.

"You used to do something dangerous," Glen summarized when they got into his duct-taped Buick Century and headed off for a two-man barbecue and all-night chess fest.

"Yes," was all Randall said. It was the only time either of them alluded to the past.

But, apparently, it was known to those who made it their business to know, and one morning the Sheriff pulled into Randall's drive, behind Glen's Century. Glen and Randall were off to the left, about two football fields away, examining the watermelon vines Randall was in the process of murdering. "What'd you do?" Glen asked Randall as they straightened, dusted off, and suspiciously eyed the approaching khaki-clad, straw-hatted, and stereotypically overweight sheriff.

"Nothing. Maybe he's here for you," Randall pointed out. Glen snorted. Not since the fifties, when he or one of his brothers was the sheriff's regular guest, accused of something heinous like self-regard.

"Mornin' gentlemen." The sheriff squinted in the sun, took off his hat, and wiped his brow, the comment including Glen because he was a new breed of lawman, or so he thought. "Hot 'un. Those going to live?" he pointed at the vines. Randall just shrugged. Glen just stood. "Well, sulfur might help. Anyways," he looked straight at Randall, "I'm wondering if I could call on your expertise."

Randall nodded, and Glen looked at him. The

sheriff turned, and Randall followed, but he stopped and gestured at Glen, “Come on.” The sheriff frowned, which was all the incentive Glen needed. He fell in step and got into the back of the patrol car, sweltering immediately because the windows didn’t roll down and the air conditioning was broken.

They drove out of Damascus to where it joined the Elba Road and made a turn on a dusty farm trail, Glen watching the vortex behind them because it was like life disappearing. They pulled into Old Man Daniel’s weedy barnyard and got out, walked past it and over a rise to see three or four men, one of them a deputy, standing over big dark lumps on the red peanut-stubbled ground. As they approached, the lumps became three dead boars.

The group around the dead boars looked up: Daniel, short, and Scot, mean and rednecky, glared at Glen, but the upset in his eyes was already saturated. One of Daniel’s sons, the one who was going to college, Joe, that’s right, moved uneasily on his feet, glad for the distraction. Glen saw why. The three boars were arranged in a circle, heads toward each other, fangs bared to the sky. Not a mark on them. Unnatural.

Randall broke the silent circle and kneeled, carefully examining each boar, duck-walking around them to pull back skin, and push at fat and hide. Took about twenty minutes, then he stood and walked around the boars in an ever-increasing spiral, his eyes locked on the ground, until he had passed around the men who watched, but said nothing, because if the sheriff brought him, then the old codger must know what he’s doing. Glen wondered a little more about Randall's past.

"What time you find 'em?" Randall asked Daniel.

"Sunrise," said in a surprised voice because, well, 'round here, work started at daybreak.

"See anything else odd?"

Daniels spat a stream of brown juice. "Ain't that odd enough?" he said, his dribbling chin taking in the boars.

Randall smiled. "Did you see anything moving? Moving away, I mean, very fast."

Daniels snorted, "They'se daid, they'se ain't moving nowhere." The set of his face conveyed how stupid he thought the question was. The set of Randall's conveyed the same sense about Daniels'. "Thanks," he said, turned, and headed back to the car.

"Thass it?" Daniels called after, incredulous, bantam-sized, and just as belligerent, and Glen eyed him as he fell in behind. "They'se blood all drained, ya know!"

"BFO," Randall muttered as Glen took his shoulder, and the sheriff hastened up, falling into step. "Coyots?" the sheriff puffed, wiping at his forehead as they made the rise and descended to the car.

"No," Randall said. "First time you've seen this, I'm betting."

"That's right."

"Any reports of missing people? Children, especially?"

"No more than usual," said as they resumed their places in the car.

"Um," Randall nodded. "Let me know when this happens again."

"It's going to happen again?" The sheriff pulled out, and the dust swirled behind, but Glen was too interested and leaned forward to listen.

"Yes," Randall said, "and, each time it does, use your GPS and start mapping the locations. And let me know, immediately, if people start disappearing. In more than the usual way," he added.

The sheriff blinked in puzzlement but knew more than Glen did about Randall's past, so said nothing. Glen didn't either, until after the sheriff dropped them off and left, and they had made their way back to the interrupted vines. "What's BFO?"

"Brilliant Flash of the Obvious," said Randall, and they returned to saving plants.

†

It did happen again, three more times, and the sheriff came for Randall, and Glen went along on two of those occasions. Boars, again, but cows on the third, arranged in a circle, drained. Rednecks chawed at the sheriff about 'gettin' a posse up for them goddamn coyots'. The sheriff looked at Randall, who just shrugged and went back home.

"You said it ain't coyote," Glen observed.

"No."

"Then, what?"

It was midday, and Randall craned a look at the molten, blazing sun. "Something very old, and very evil."

A younger man would have responded with incredulity or demanded explanations, but Glen had seen plenty over the years. "What we gonna do?"

Randall smiled at Glen's inclusion. "Hope we get it before it gets us."

The sun was just horrid, but Glen felt the cold rise in his soul. "We in trouble?"

Randall stopped smiling. "Yes."

†

That very night, as it turned out. Glen was in a deep sleep, one filled with terrible images, the kind Maw Maw used to call 'h'aint touch,' when something dead made an effort at your soul. The dread forced Glen out of his sleep and paralyzed him as he realized the h'aint was still there. Right outside his bedroom window.

It was riding waves of moonlight and piling against the glass. It wanted in. There was a crack in the window, and given how liquid the thing was, it should have oozed through. But it didn't. It wanted help. It wanted Glen to get out of bed, open the window, and help it over the sill.

Which is exactly what Glen found himself doing moments later. "What the hell?" he asked himself as he fumbled at catches and handles. Took an effort to stop, and whatever pressed against the glass sorrowed and wept, and Glen felt so sorry for it that he reached again.

"No," Maw Maw's voice whispered in his ear.

"Yes," something cold and soulless whispered after.

Glen slid to the floor, hands still grasping at the window, and lay there the rest of the night with angels and devils battling for control, until there was a beam of sunrise and the cold, mournful thing shrieked and was gone.

Glen cried, then fell asleep.

When he woke, it was mid-morning. "Randall," he whispered.

Glen made it to Randall's in about five minutes. The front door was open. He found Randall curled up beside the bed, blankets pulled over him to keep out the light. It took quite an effort to rouse him, and Randall, pale, eyes completely black, no cornea, smiled mournfully, "I wasn't as strong as you," he whispered.

Glen hauled him back into bed and draped him because the sunlight hurt Randall. "What do we do?" he asked.

"We have to find it, put a hawthorn stake through its heart, cut off its head, stuff that with garlic, then burn its hiding place."

"Hawthorn? Ain't none of that around here."

Randall glanced at a cabinet. Glen opened it and found everything. "What did you used to do?" he asked, but Randall didn't answer, cocked a dead eye toward the front of his house instead. "Sheriff's here," he said.

"Well, good mornin'." The sheriff looked surprised to see Glen open the door, and Glen knew Davis's 'old queers' comment was running through his head, but the sheriff believed he was a new type of lawman, so didn't express it. "Is Mr. Morris in?"

"He's sick."

"Hmm, you ain't lookin' too good yourself." The sheriff pushed his hat back. BFO, Glen thought. "Well, I got those coordinates for him." He had an envelope in his hand.

"I can get it to him." Glen reached, but the sheriff hesitated, because new lawman or no, redneckery died hard. Glen ended up pulling it from his fingers to a flash of 'Boy, who you think you are?' in the sheriff's eyes, but he remembered he was new breed and gave it up. “Hope he’s feelin’ better,” he said as he once-overed Glen and, no doubt, was back on the ‘queers’ thought. “Oh, and tell him a couple of kids have disappeared, one of them Joe Daniels.” The sheriff left.

“Where is this?” Randall pointed at the part of the county map where lines and numbers converged. Glen examined it, then sucked in his breath. “Cryman’s,” he whispered. “It’s the Cryman’s Hole.”

“What’s that?” Randall’s voice was a dead leaf skittering in the wind.

“Cryman comes outta his hole at night, looking for kids to eat. This where he lives.” Glen stabbed the map. “It’s a set of deep ravines, all switching back on each other.”

“So, this has been happening here for a while?”

“No, ain’t never happened. Was just a story the old folk told us kids to scare us and keep us outta that place. It’s dangerous.”

“So it knew the story and took advantage.” Randall didn’t have to explain what ‘it’ was. “You have to get me out there.”

“Why?”

“Because,” a voice out of skulls, out of darkness, “I’ll know exactly where it’s sleeping.”

“How?”

Randall didn’t say anything.

“I mean, how do I get you out there?” The sun was too hurtful.

“When the sun is the highest, I’ll be okay. For an hour.”

“That ain’t enough time.”

“Bring these blankets so you can wrap me up

when the hour is over."

Glen nodded. Gathered everything. Got ready.

†

Somewhere at noon, Randall sprang out of bed, strong, eyes clear. "Let's go," he said. Glen, who'd fortified himself with coffee and Jack, rushed him outside, but Randall had to stop for a moment and push a deadening face to the sun, just for a moment. "Ah," he whispered, "Goodbye," and they piled into the Century and whipped out of the yard.

Glen raced down the road and two-wheeled it onto Stewart's back trail, smacking open the cow gate with the bumper and bouncing the shockless car over the wash, Randall actually laughing with the sport of it, until they crested a knoll. "There," Glen pointed.

The land fell in layers, each covered with increasingly thick pine until the lowest was impenetrable. A mist hung over that part. Shouldn't be.

The road ended in boulders, and they could drive no farther. Randall sprang from the car, vital, twenty years old again, and life blasted from him in waves of power. "Ah!" he screamed to the sun, at apogee, his arms out and embracing. He whirled on Glen. Those eyes.

Glen stepped back, fumbling for the cross around his neck. "Randall!"

Randall blinked, regarding him as an owl regards a mouse. He smiled, something lupine about it, and took a step forward. Glen shrank against the bumper. "If you could just FEEL this."

The gloat and frenzy on his face smacked Glen to the ground.

"Just FEEL it!" Randall roared, ancient and dark, reaching out ...

And stopped.

"No," Randall whispered, covering his face with his hands. "You won't have me. You won't have us."

Glen watched the fight for Randall's soul, clutching the cross, which was more a comfort to him than a weapon during this Magic Hour. Randall fell to his knees, fingers that now bore claws tearing at his face, but there was no blood. Precious minutes passed before Randall gasped and staggered back to his feet, still twenty years old, but no longer voracious. "We're running out of time," he pointed at thc sun. "Come on." And he bolted for the woods.

Glen was not twenty years old and slowed by the equipment, gasped his way in the hot air, losing sight of Randall in seconds; but he knew where he was going. When he got there, the chill stopped him. Unnatural. H'aint touched. Gloomy from the Spanish moss like a weave across the top of the pines, but no way even a deep hole like this was so cold.

Randall stood at the entrance to the Cryman's, a narrow gap where two ravines almost touched. He was combative, because, standing in the entrance itself, was Joe Daniels. Or what used to be Joe.

"The Master calls you," the Joe thing hissed at Randall, and then glared past him at Glen. His sudden grin slavered into spit and old blood. "And you bring meat!" He took a predator's step—Glen paralyzed by the sheer evil blasting from Joe's eyes.

Randall struck Joe a blow so fast and vicious, Glen could barely follow it.

Joe's head exploded into flesh shreds, and he bounced off the ravine wall, an animal scream ripping from his lips. "You hurt me!" Joe wailed, trying to put his scalp back together.

"You are not turned," Randall said to him, "Get out of my way, and you'll be saved."

Joe cowered in the entrance. "I don't want salvation," he moaned, but did nothing as Randall stepped over him. Glen hesitated, certain Joe would rip him apart, but all he did was nurse his torn scalp as Glen pushed past, not even looking up. That's what slavery does to you.

The Hole was dark, not only from the moss-woven trees, but because the light fled. Turned its back, more accurately. The Hole widened out, forming almost a bowl, then came back on itself at the far end to another narrow entrance, the place where the Cryman slept. Randall was in the middle, at the widest part, stock still. He was staring at the Cryman's Rest because something was there. Something insubstantial.

It was like a mist trying to form. Vaguely human, it wouldn't define itself, just shimmered in and out of view, a cloud of fireflies trying to coordinate their flashes, but failing. Cold came off it in waves, as if from the bottom of a newly dug grave. Glen gasped and took a step back as the waves hammered him. He never knew that air could lust like that.

"Don't run," Randall put out a warning hand, somehow reading Glen's intent. "You'll never make it." He was fixed on the mist, concentrating, a pulse between it and Randall, talk between distant birds. From the set of Randall's shoulders, he was losing the discussion. Glen's hands crept up to the cross.

"No," Randall's voice was a whisper in his ear, although he had not turned, and there was no indication he spoke. "That won't do you any good. Magic Hour," and the voice indicated up, above the moss weave, and Glen took an involuntary glance. They were still within noon, the spot of light marking the sun edging a fraction more off-center.

"Shoot it," the voice whispered as the pulse between Randall and the mist grew in intensity, and the mist moved off the Cryman's Door, coming for Randall.

Shoot a mist. Glen reached into his pocket and pulled out the .45 he'd kept after the Korean War. The mist stretched and sloped into a somewhat human shape as it reached out for Randall, who opened up for embrace. Glen put two rounds into what he figured was the heart. The mist screamed, roiling into itself, and Glen shot it two more times. More screams, nothing human in them, the plaintive cry of something desperate to live.

The mist fell, heavy, onto the red clay, and then rolled, wounded, back through the Cryman's Door, whimpering. Joe, somewhere behind them, unleashed an agonizing wail of grief. Randall collapsed.

Glen, instantly beside him, pulled him up by the shoulders. "No," Randall gasped, "we're not done. You're not done." He pointed at the Door. "Go in there. You'll find it in a hole toward the back. Stake it through the heart. Cut off its head. Stuff the mouth with the garlic. Scatter the earth you find it resting on. Then burn the body." That last nothing but a wheeze, and Randall folded into a fetal position.

Go in there? Glen stared at the Cryman's Door, a place he'd never had the courage to enter when he was a brazen, big-mouthed ten-year-old. Malevolence oozed from it. Anger, too.

"Go," Randall whispered, "or we'll all die. Or worse, never die."

It was, as Randall said, buried in a hole in the back where sunlight could not reach. Randall had not warned him about the three children scattered around the hole, their throats torn out. Glen recognized one of them as part of the Chapman brood from off toward Elba, and that made him mad because they were good kids.

"You sonofabitch," he snarled as he swept back the covering dirt and stared at the thing. It looked human—some white man dressed in a shirt and slacks—the four holes from the .45 arranged around its torso and spouting black chunks of what used to be blood. The eyes weren't human, though. Not at all.

"Don't look at it!" Randall's whisper in his ear ... but, those eyes. So ancient. So lifeless, the eyes of a wolf forever in stalk, centuries of murder and hunting pooled in blood and singing with the joy of it. The scent and the pursuit and the terror and the ungodly ecstasy of the fear and dominance and you are all mine, you are prey, fall before me ...

Glen slid to his knees, the monster's eyes triumphant and paralyzing him. Master, I serve, I am for you. Randall's whispers frantic, but unintelligible now, and the Master sat up, his fangs bared, his arms reached ...

And its eyes said, hurry, we are running out of time.

Glen's head snapped up.

"You sure are, you bastard," and he struck the stake hard and true, and the thing screamed and screamed and clawed and tore at him as he hammered and hammered until it was pinned to the clay hole and he tore off its head with the machete and slammed that onto the still-moving torso and yanked open the teeth that still tried to bite him and stuffed it with the garlic and reached down and scattered the black, blood-drenched earth the thing settled on and squeezed out the lighter fluid and dropped the match ...

It went up like paper. Old and dead and dry, writhing in more flame than Glen could have caused, the burning arms trying to put the head back in its place but the fire, invested, turned blue, stinking of sulfur and the Pit, and there was one last scream and a roar and an explosion of sparks that dazzled Glen. And it was gone.

"Help me." Randall's whisper in his ear. Glen rushed out. Randall was still curled on the clay, a hand raised, finger pointing at the sun.

Magic Hour was over.

"Dammit!" Glen rushed to him as purifying sunlight sought Randall, and he began to smoke. Glen wrapped him in the blanket, tight, throwing on the comforter to cover exposed flesh, laying on top of him. "It'll be fine, it'll be fine," he spoke through the layers.

"Get me out of here," a burnt whisper pleaded.

Glen helped the bundle to its feet, shuffling along. Joe was gone, his screams diminishing in the distance. He got Randall out of the Cryman's and up the levels to the plain, the car just ahead, blazing in the full sun. “We’re almost there,” he whispered to the blankets.

A surge of movement, and Glen was flung to the ground, barely missing the front bumper and a good crack on the head. He spun on the wiregrass and saw the blankets standing tall and strong. With purpose.

“I cannot live like this,” Randall called out.

“No,” Glen said.

“I cannot.” A pause, mournful. “I can’t become one.” A surge of motion, blankets flung away.

“No!” Glen scrambled to his feet, but he was too late.

As if the sun was horrified at what it beheld—a crimson-eyed Randall, black veins popped along his entire face, squirming worms desperate for blood, and teeth poked through his lips like a wild boar’s—the sun slapped him down hard, pouring an avalanche of fire and light over the obscenity Randall had become and cleansing, cleansing. White-hot light burst out from Randall’s chest and he screamed; an agony of hellfire and damnation washed over Glen with a heat seven times that of a flame and loss so profound, so eternal, he fell to the ground in horror, lonely. Forever.

When Glen came to, it was the hour before sunset, and he was unmarked. No burns, no wounds, except something had seared him down to his bones, which were, strangely, cold. He staggered to his feet and braced against the bumper, gasping for air and trying to warm the cold thing deep within, but it did not respond. Never would.

The blankets lay piled before him, and, gingerly, Glen approached, pushed them aside with a stick.

Nothing but some ash piled up like an offering, with what might be a tooth fragment in the middle. Glen sobbed, looked up at the sun going down, kicked at the pile viciously, jumped in the car, and drove as if the hounds of hell pursued, back to his house.

Where he stayed, a peculiar old Black man, dismissed as unimportant and worthless, for the rest of his days. He never ventured out at night. You'd see him peering out between the curtains from time to time, and swear, *swear*, there was something moving on the edge of the woods. But nobody ever checked.

COME LIVE WITH US
FOREVER

Come Live with Us Forever

They pulled the little boy's body out of the pond about two hours after they'd started the search. The boy's mother had been nearby and saw, and screamed and screamed, and that was unfortunate, just unfortunate.

"Dammit," Sheriff Zimm muttered and strode over to detach the woman from the soggy body, but she was having none of it.

"Barry! Barry!" she screamed.

Zimm looked up at his two deputies, Carla and Roland, and made a 'fucking help me here!' face, and they both reached under the woman's arms and tried to pull her off, but she wasn't having any of it. This was turning into a circus.

Maybe if you'd kept a better eye on your kid ...

An utterly uncharitable thought, and he was immediately ashamed of it, but he couldn't have this caterwauling while the coroner's people and the search people stood by, gaping. He looked about for more help. The woman's father, Morgan Reed, the kid's grandfather, stood to the side, shock on his face. "You want to help us here, Mr. Reed?"

Morgan snapped out of his paralysis, glanced at Zimm, walked over, and said gentle things that Zimm couldn't quite make out. This, more than any effort by the three officers, loosened her grip on the body. She sagged into her father's arms, and he took her back to the farmhouse, each step an agony, and Zimm's heart broke. She was a woman devastated. He looked down at the little boy, foam in his mouth, black eyes wide open, soaked red hair down the side of his face. This was a devastating loss.

Which would be disposed of with the efficiency of established systems: coroners and ambulances, an autopsy later and then the remains to the funeral home, the only one in Seneca Top, and laid to rest with the whole town, or what's left of them, attending.

Tragedy was currency in small towns.

Zimm went to his car, Carla and Roland following. He'd arrived after them and parked behind, basically trapping their squad car until he decided to go back to the office. He waited for the searchers and others to gather their things and get to their respective vehicles, nodding or shaking their heads as they passed him and saying the usual things you expect when there's tragedy:

"Damn shame."

"Cute little boy."

"Terrible when these things happen."

And then they were all gone. He looked at his deputies. "So what's the story here?" he said from the space between the cars.

The deputies exchanged looks and shrugged. "The Mom was screaming that her boy was missing from his room, that someone had taken him, and Morgan called us and we all showed up and ..." Helpless gesture at the pond.

"Did someone take him?" Oh no, not a custody

battle gone wrong.

"Not as far as we can see. Morgan said he heard Bumpy's voice right before she woke him, but that had to be a dream." Carla said.

"Bumpy?"

"Bumpy Laroux, boy's father."

"Bumpy is his real name?"

She nodded. Zimm shook his head. Parents can be cruel.

"He got killed in a prison fight a few months ago." She gestured at the pond. "So couldn't be him."

Ya think? "So what's the story with her?"

"Not much of one. The mother's name is Cathy. Morgan is her grandfather."

Hmm. Got that wrong. Morgan looked too young. Come to think of it, so did Cathy.

"She's from Uvalde, which is about three towns over—"

"I know where it is." He cut Roland short.

Another exchange of looks, "Uh, well, sorry, I wasn't sure," Roland, grudgingly.

Zimm felt a slow burn. "Okay, I know you're not exactly thrilled with my appointment, that both of you think either of you should have filled the position,"—not so surreptitious glances at each other—"but that'll be remedied with the next election, when either of you can stand, if you choose." He looked between them: they remained impassive. "In the meantime, I'm here, at the commissioner's request, until relieved." Another pause. "And I studied a map before I got here."

"Alright, sure. Sorry." Pause. "Sheriff." This from Carla, who Zimm had immediately pegged as the smarter and more ambitious of the six deputies assigned to the office. And the most devious. He gestured for her to go on.

"She was always trouble. In school, out. Her parents disowned her, and she took up with Bumpy."

"That's why she was here? Her man got sent away?"

"Morgan's about the only relative she's got who puts up with her."

"Why's that?"

Roland shrugged, taking over the narrative. "He's a decent guy. Sort of a Jesus freak, but good for all that."

Zimm gazed at the house and wondered what a decent old man could do for a wayward granddaughter who had lost everything in just a few short weeks. Maybe he can bring her to Jesus. "So everyone's been notified, then?"

"Not the Laroux."

"You taking care of that?" he asked Carla point-blank. Whatever sexism anyone wanted to attach to it, female officers were better at delivering bad news than the male ones. She frowned and cast troubled eyes at Roland, who looked away. "What?"

"Well, the Laroux ... they're a problem."

"I gathered that from their son, Bumpy. And the fact they named him Bumpy."

No reaction, which confirmed Zimm's conviction that neither of them had a sense of humor. "We've had to arrest them lots of times." Carla paused. "So they don't particularly like us." Hand wave between her and Roland.

"But they know you." Zimm pointed out,

implying that it would be a familiar visit for the Laroux.

"But they *don't* know you. So they'd be more receptive."

Good point, maybe. But Zimm wasn't completely buying it. "Even though I'm driving a county car?"

They both nodded, and Zimm saw what this was: a test for him, and a way for them to get out of an unpleasant duty. Well played, deputy. "Where are they located?"

"Bottom of Top, at the side road off 618 at Robert's Gas Station. They're at the end of the gravel road." Zimm had studied his map enough to know the directions, and he gave them both an appraising look before he went to his car.

"They're Senecas," Roland called after him, and he turned and looked at him with true bafflement.

"Right. They live in Seneca Top."

"No." Roland waved that away. "They're real Senecas. Indians."

"What does that mean?"

"They're ... different."

Zimm wasn't sure if he was hearing a racist remark, which was odd coming from a Hispanic like Roland, but Carla was nodding in agreement. He would have liked to ask them to elaborate, but maybe it was best he found out for himself. After all, he had five more months in this shithole before he could retire. Finally.

It wasn't Zimm's fault that the elected sheriff of this county keeled over with a heart attack last month, and that the commissioner didn't like the deputy sheriff who should have taken over, a slug named Whittaker, who apparently never came to work. But he did like Zimm, who, at this point in his rapidly dissolving career, was riding a desk outside the commissioner's office. Not that Zimm particularly enjoyed riding a desk; he'd been a street guy for twenty-eight years, but a man has to know his limitations (as one particularly good movie cop said once), and Zimm had realized his four years prior. Took him two years to get to the desk job, and was all set to ride that to retirement when the commissioner made him an offer he couldn't refuse.

So here he was.

It was actually a step up from the desk because this was a quiet county, mostly, with the usual small group of idiots doing 90% of the crime, and routine to scoop up the usual small group of idiots whenever a burglary, car theft, or meth lab, surfaced. He supposed these Laroux were in that category, Seneca or not.

A shack at the end of the gravel road and, even then, Zimm considered the term charitable. It was almost impossible to see where the lichen-covered boards and plywood ended and the surrounding jungle began. It was like the house and woods were growing into each other, or the shack was the fruit of the trees. And what was with this pseudo-jungle terrain? This was cold country; high elevation and swamps shouldn't really exist here. Some vagary of geography, he supposed, an offshoot of the big river that bordered this county, mercifully separating it from the more civilized lands to the south. Like his place.

The yard, if you could call it that, was littered with the expected stock of rusted car chassis, refrigerators, and unidentifiable piles of metal overtaken by poison ivy and every other noxious vine that a swamp produced. Typical. Zimm didn't know if yard neglect was a characteristic of the criminal class, or a deliberate warning to any intruders, including law enforcement, that difficult people lived here.

"Hello!" Zimm called at what appeared to be the front door, but who knows, could just be a fault in the plywood. He stayed by the front of his car because it gave immediate cover should someone come blasting their way out, and quick getaway should something less than human appear.

"Hello!" he called again. Oh, please come out, blasting or subhuman or no, because he really didn't want to walk on that rotting green-slimed porch.

There was a shuffling at the door, and it somehow opened, not so much swinging on hinges as parting. An old woman stepped over the threshold. 'Old woman' was, again, charitable because, good Lord. Didn't look a day over 100, and didn't look like a brush had been through that tangled bird's nest of gray-washed, but still extraordinarily thick, mophead hair since probably 90 of that 100. All Zimm could see of her face were two black-lit eyes peering at him through gaps in the tresses. 'Course that may be more due to the rest of her features swallowed by her very dark skin, almost black. Were Senecas dark-skinned? He supposed. There were mostly Mohawks around Zimm's home county, and they ranged from indistinguishable Caucasians, to some pretty dark characters. "Is this the Laroux home?" he called to her.

"We already know." The voice that carried to him was fingernails on chalkboard, bones scraped by metal files, and he swore, could swear, it was several voices blended together. He took an inadvertent step back and almost chided himself for cowardice. Almost. "*What* do you know?"

"The boy. We know. He's back with his family."

"What?" Zimm had heard her clearly, her voice a drill in the ear, but that didn't make sense.

The old woman made an impatient gesture, the flour sack dress falling down her arm and revealing a shriveled thing that was best described by the word, 'dug.' How revolting. "We got the boy back, I said. He's ours. The Water Spirit saved him from that whore." She spat something green onto the porch, which explained the color. "That whore. She think she can keep what's ours?" She spat again.

"I have no idea what you're talking about."

She smiled. Ghastly. A broken picket fence framed by the greasy hair locks. "You will." And melted back into the house.

Zimm figured this was a good time to leave.

"What do you know about Seneca Water Spirits?" he asked Carla when he got back. She was typing up the last of the necessary reports. That's the problem with police work, the always necessary reports.

She looked at him blankly. "What?"

"Know anything about them?"

She shrugged. "Never heard of it." And she resumed typing.

"It's the reason the Seneca live up here," a voice behind him. Zimm turned, and it was Colley, the ancient dispatcher who ran the desk. Actually, Colley wasn't that much more ancient than Zimm, so they'd established an immediate old-man rapport.

"Okay." Zimm nodded for him to continue.

Colley grinned and sipped his coffee as Carla rolled her eyes in opinion of Colley's mental encyclopedia of useless facts that he would spout given any provocation. "The Water Snake poisoned their homes, down where you're from, so they prayed to their Thunders, and he led them up here where the water's too fast for the Snake, and they've lived here peacefully ever since."

"Okay." Zimm figured this was the Cliff Notes version of the legend. "So the Water Snake's an enemy."

"Not for the witches."

"Pardon?"

"The Seneca witches. *Dagwaoneneyent.*"

"Pardon?"

"They live forever. They're pretty evil."

Carla's eye roll had almost forced its way through her head, but Zimm could sympathize. He may have just met one.

"Sheriff?"

Colley over the radio. Probably wanted to go to lunch. As though they were so busy, anyone would notice his absence. Last few days since the boy drowned, nothing but some stolen mail and a fender bender. Indeed, Zimm was parked out here on the bypass looking for speeders, to keep himself awake more than anything. “Go,” he called back.

“Got some trouble at the Reed place.”

Uh oh. “What kind of trouble?”

“DB.” Pause. “Maybe a 10-56.”

Oh no. A dead body, a suicide. The mother. “On my way.”

Even with lights and sirens, it took him ten minutes. Carla and Roland were down by the pond, standing on either side of a sheet-covered body, the old man, Reed, standing at its head, all three of them looking down at it. Zimm took all this in as he stepped down the incline and put his hand on Reed’s shoulder. “Mr. Reed, best you go back to the house.”

“I found her.”

“I know. We’ll take your statement, but I need to see the body, and I don’t want to make this worse for you.”

“I seen it already.”

Zimm paused. “Very well,” and he nodded at Roland who, gingerly, pulled the sheet back halfway. The girl, water-soaked and no longer pretty, but not a suicide. Oh no. Not with that great gaping wound in her chest, another one in her stomach.

He looked up sharply at Reed, ready to stuff and cuff him, but he stood there swaying a little, expression unreadable, and there was no murder in him. Only grief. “What happened, Mr. Reed?”

“Them Laroux. They got her.”

“Did you see them, Mr. Reed?”

His glare transferred from the body to Zimm. “Didn’t have to see them.”

Not exactly prosecutable, but there was that threat from the *dagnabit* or whatever the hell Colley had called the Laroux witch, and that was good enough for some follow-up. In force.

“Roland,” he said, “stay here. See if you can find the weapon. Carla, with me,” and he headed to his car.

Ten minutes later, he pulled up to the rotted swamp-water house. “Get the shotgun,” he said to Carla, who was almost too eager to get it off the rack. He had to give her a warning look because they didn’t have anything but suspicion at this point.

He stepped to the front of the car and called out, “Mrs. Laroux!”

A thrashing in the woods to the left of the house, and Zimm had the startled thought that a bear was coming through but, no. A human. Sort of.

A man. Sort of. Six and a half feet tall and wide, maybe even taller and wider, shirt off, revealing a mass of tangled muscles promising the ability to rip off a sheriff’s arms should the monster so choose, skin as dark as the old lady’s and hair down the shoulders, blackly luxuriant. Would have made a good Conan stand-in. “Watchew want?”

"Stele," Carla whispered, the shotgun held tight and, boy, was he glad she had it. Although he wasn’t sure it would stop that thing.

“Stelly? Is that some kind of Seneca name?” he whispered back.

“No, it’s like some tall carved stone or something.”

Oh. Stele. Fitting.

Zimm considered his next move, one that wouldn't get him eaten. "I want you to come down to the station for questioning." Bravado was called for when faced with overwhelming odds, Zimm had discovered over the years.

The monster laughed. "Questioning for what?"

"The murder of Cathy Reed."

A slow smile appeared on Stele's face, like a crack in a rock. "Weren't no murder. Was righteousness."

"What?" Zimm stared at him blankly.

"You Laroux, you always Laroux, you live with us forever. Don't matter." He made a contemptuous gesture to the side. "No matter."

"What in the flying hell are you talking about?"

The monster glowered at Zimm. "You're new here."

"I am. And I cordially invite you to get in the back of this car and accompany us to the station, where you can give me a full briefing about this situation of the Laroux that requires everyone to live with you forever." And Zimm dropped his hand to his pistol. And Carla shifted the shotgun to the ready. Trembling, Zimm noted. The eagerness was gone. She was genuinely frightened.

And a moment later, he knew why.

Two more monsters emerged from the woods and flanked Stele, both of them equally muscled and long-haired and dark-skinned and maybe even taller and broader. Goliath and his brothers.

"That's the twins." Carla's voice shook. "Huey and Dewey."

"You're kidding me, right?"

She wasn't. "There's another one, a younger brother."

"Louie?"

She nodded.

"Great. So we can expect him to join the party?"

"No, he's in Dannamora."

Thank the Lord for small favors.

Stele grinned at them and then gave his brothers significant looks. "I like the way this one talks." He pointed at Zimm. The twins grunted their agreement. Zimm figured their entire vocabulary consisted of grunts.

"Gentlemen," Zimm said with all the world weariness he could muster, to cover his alarm and growing dread, "I am not in a very good mood. I am not going to try to *persuade* you to accompany us, so get in the car, or I will shoot all three of you in the legs and pile you in the back." He unsnapped his holster.

The three gave him the most malevolent of shared looks, and Stele said. "We all won't fit in the back."

"Just you, then."

"You got a warrant?"

Well, no, he didn't, and he should have realized these three, this entire clan, was so familiar with the legal process that they could probably pass the bar on the first try.

Stele took the response from Zimm's face and smiled triumphantly. "Come back when you do," and he and his two brothers turned and disappeared into the woods in similar fashion to the way their witch mother—grandmother?—had blended into the house.

A gasp of relief from behind, and Zimm turned to see Carla sweating and still pale. He looked at the shotgun and wondered if that would have been enough. “Do we have tranquilizer rifles?” he asked.

She blinked. “We can get ’em from Forestry. They use them on bears.”

He nodded. “We’ll bring those next time.”

The coroner said two stab wounds, heart and lower abdomen, delivered with great force, the heart wound almost through to the back. Zimm could think of at least one person in the vicinity who looked as though he could deliver a knife blow hard enough to go all the way through. Especially if he had help from twin monsters.

“Funny thing,” the coroner said, “wasn't a knife. Looked more like some kind of big ice pick.”

“A big ice pick?”

“Yes.” Dr Junger, a shriveled old dyspeptic former state pathologist living out his last years in a bywater, probably avoiding some earlier scandal that Zimm just didn’t want to know about. “The wounds are round and no tears. Very smooth, like …” His voice trailed off.

“Like?”

“A walrus tusk or something like that.”

“A tusk.” Zimm looked at him skeptically. “I guess the next thing you’re going to say is, ‘like a giant water serpent’.”

Junger tsked. “Well, no, that would just be silly. But there’s lots of hunting around here and lots of antlers available.”

“You saying this was done by antlers?”

Shrug. “Something bigger. And, no, not a giant water serpent.”

Zimm shook his head. This was crazy. “Is it a ritual?”

Shrug.

“Maybe, uh, some kind of revenge ritual. You ever hear of anything like that?”

“No, not really. Some of the tribes around here use antlers and other big animal bones for some of their ceremonies, but I never heard of a revenge one.”

“Like, who, the Senecas?”

He shrugged. “I suppose.”

Well, Christ on a crutch, this was just enough information to harden his suspicions and get laughed right out of the judge’s chamber. Needed more. He left the coroner’s and headed straight to the Reed farm. Morgan Reed was sitting on his porch in the gathering dusk, facing the pond. Staring at it.

“Tell me what happened,” Zimm said as he approached.

“I told you, it was the Laroux.”

“What did you see?”

“Nothin’. I was asleep. Saw her layin’ down there when I stepped out to get a cigarette.” He stopped, his face working. “They called her down there.”

“Who called her?”

“Barry.”

“What?”

“No. Not actually him. Them.”

“Who’s them?”

Reed turned a baleful eye on him. “You know who.”

Yes, yes, he did. “I need proof, Mr. Reed. Something that’ll convince a judge to give me a warrant. I know what kind of weapon I’m looking for—”

“Weapon?” Reed interrupted, blinking in surprise. “Weren’t no weapon.”

Zimm raised eyebrows, asking the question. “Ain’t no weapon you can bring into court, anyways. It’s them.” His eyebrows lowered, “You will not suffer a witch to live.”

Zimm’s eyebrows remained at nadir. “You’re not planning to do something stupid, are you, Morgan?”

He sniffed and reached under his rocking chair, produced a Bowie knife, and pulled a whetstone, and began working it as Zim’s alarm subsided and he took his hand off his pistol. “Question stands, Morgan.”

“Not to them.” The contempt in his voice identified the witch and her giant sons. “It.”

“It?”

Reed pointed at the pond, now murky with the twilight. “What lives down there.”

“I’m not following, Morgan.”

“The demon. What they called up. Takes souls, lives with it forever.” Pause. “In hell.”

Zimm blinked and studied the old man. “I’m thinking I need to take you to the hospital, Morgan.”

“I’m perfectly fine.”

“I don’t think you are.”

“Got a warrant?”

Second time today ... man, the general populace was savvy. “I can get one.” Which he knew was as empty a threat as it sounded.

Morgan snorted. “I’ll be done by then.”

“With what?”

This time, the blade pointed at the water. “It.”

“Commissioner, I’m just not all that certain I can last this tour.” A surreptitious phone conversation, because Zimm didn’t want Colley overhearing this. Didn’t want anyone overhearing this.

“Now, Bill,” the patient, solicitous voice of his boss, “it’s less than four months now, and as soon as they have their elections, you can go back to your wife.” Snigger. Everyone knew Zimm and Mrs. Weren’t exactly getting along, another reason why this six-month tour had been appealing. The commissioner gave the other appealing reason. “This’ll really bump your retirement pay, too, more field service, more time in grade. So what’s the problem?”

“These people are insane, boss.”

“Most people are. But that desk work was driving *you* insane.” Solicitous chuckle. “I may have had to force you into earlier retirement.”

“At this point, I would welcome that.”

Moments of silence on the other side, as the boss man calculated how much this recalcitrant employee was inconveniencing him. Zimm knew what the boss did to subordinates who inconvenienced him.

“Is it that bad?” Conveying a degree of ridicule. A mature, streetwise, very experienced law-enforcement master like Zimm couldn't handle a tad of crazy?

“Witches and water serpents. Revenge from

beyond the grave. Mutant siblings and a clan that believes family is forever." He paused. "Even after they're dead."

Solicitous chuckle. "C'mon, Bill, you've seen stuff like this before."

"Yeah. But, I didn't believe it before."

That pretty much ended the conversation and Zimm knew he had stepped on it big time, but his willies were increasing with each passing day. A crime like this leaves its traces ... guys like him found those traces and cataloged and studied them and presented evidence to convict killers, even if they're half-crazed witch people. But there's no evidence. No trace. Nothing he can bag and tag. And that makes no sense.

He grabbed his hat. "I'm going out," he said as he passed Colley doing a crossword puzzle. "Okay, boss." Wave of a pencil. "I'll let you know if the commissioner calls back."

Zimm let out a long sigh. He should have known better than to think anything was private anymore. No doubt, this conversation will be roundly discussed by Carla and Roland, and half the town.

He drove out to Reed's place. Always start at the scene, no matter how many times you have to go back. He pulled up and honked the horn, but Reed did not emerge.

"Mr. Reed?" he called as he walked up on the porch. The door was open and he knocked and called, but no response. He stepped inside to an early 1970s décor of shag rug, wing chairs, a velvet Jesus over the woodstove, and, good Lord, a lava lamp? Chuckling, he went back outside. The old man was probably sleeping. Or drunk.

Can you blame him?

He took the path toward the pond and, as he drew closer, slowed. What's that? On the edge. A ... shotgun? He hustled to it and, yeah, double-barreled, at least a .12 if not bigger, half in and out of the water. And blood on the grass. And big drag marks from the shore, disappearing into the muddy pond. And a big shiny thing ... he picked it up. Slimy, translucent.

A giant fish scale.

He pulled the radio off his belt, called, and after what seemed like an eternity but was actually only a few minutes later, everyone came: deputies, firefighters, emergency personnel, even the rangers. Any excitement in a dull place brought out the troops.

"He's down there?" The Fire Marshal, Ben Something-or-other, pointed at the pond.

"Yes."

The Marshal shook his head. "Take us a while to get some divers, some boats."

Zimm looked up and spotted the wheel and gate at the other end of the pond. "Drain it," he said.

The Marshal blinked twice at him, tapped one of his firemen, and headed off to do just that. Oh boy, water dispersal, a fireman's dream.

It took all night. Zimm stayed right there the whole time, ordering Carla and Roland and the rest of the deputies to go about their business—the county's business, really—and he would take watch. They grumbled because they wanted to be in on this, too, but left and it was him at the edge of the pond as it got lower and lower. The shotgun rested on the exposed bank and the blood had dissipated with the receding water; a couple of firemen monitored the gate and looked at him across the way like he was crazy or something.

At dawn, he stared through a couple of feet of murky water left below the gate's opening. Catfish and carp flopped here and there, and the bottom grass lay over. And ...

... Reed. Torn almost in half. One intact arm, his hand grasping the hilt of the Bowie knife. Which was driven through the bony throat of a serpent skeleton. With long, boney fangs. And boney wings on its head.

Zimm retired that day.

ATTITUDE
ADJUSTMENT

Attitude Adjustment

Lordy, Marla thought as the guy came through the door, if that isn't someone absolutely out of place. Skinny, bit of a pot belly, highwater jeans and white sneakers, black-rimmed glasses, acne, a formal button-down shirt with a green t-shirt underneath ... oh my God, was there a *Dungeons & Dragons* convention nearby? And didn't the choppers parked wheel to wheel outside give him a clue?

The Macheteros were just as surprised as she was, twenty or twenty-five of them lining the bar and the pool table and the stripper stage, all turning about, as if on signal, to stare at the dweeb. Even Candy Cane flipped backward off the pole and stared. The Macheteros blinked in unison, as if the same simple thought raced through their tiny brains: what the fuck is this loser doing in here? Followed by a unified suspicion, because this had classic cop setup written all over it, although Marla doubted the dweeb had any affiliation with any kind of law enforcement. No department was that desperate.

The dweeb blinked, pushed his glasses back on his face, and shuffled forward, studiously avoiding Crowbar and Sloppy Seconds and Chainlink, who were closest to the door playing pinfinger with their Bowie knives, which they stopped as the dweeb went past, staring open-mouthed at him. He ran the gauntlet of the other members who followed his progress to the middle of the bar, where Marla stood, Mike and Crewcut sitting in front of her. Both of them got up, made exaggerated bows to the dweeb, and flourished hands at the bar stool. “Please, be our guest!” Mike announced.

“Thank you,” the dweeb said, his voice as squeaky as one expected. That broke the surprise, and the whole bar burst out laughing, slapping each other on the back, thoroughly enjoying themselves. Candy did a back somersault to the pole, which earned her much appreciation, and most everyone returned to their amusements. Most everyone.

Mike and Crewcut remained behind the dweeb as Marla leaned forward, not caring that her tits almost popped out of her leather vest. Girl’s gotta make her tips, and, who knows, this dweeb might be appreciative. Which, based on his saucer eyes and dropped jaw, indicated he was, and she smiled to herself. If she ever wanted to actually get that tip money, then she should try to save this idiot's life. “Do you have any idea where you are?”

Still fixed on her tits, which she knew were spectacular, the dweeb nodded and squeaked. “Yes. It’s a bar called the Pig Knuckle.”

“Very good. You can read signs. Do you have any idea what this place is?”

“I presume it's a place that serves alcohol and has female entertainment.” Said with eyes still tit-rapt, while jamming a thumb back toward Candy.

Mike and Crewcut, who were listening closely, busted up at that, looking at each other with great hilarity. Which was not good.

"Let me help you out," Marla insisted. "This is the favorite bar of the Macheteros Motorcycle Club. Do you know who they are?"

"I'm presuming it's this group of gentlemen and the occasional lady,"—a sweep of the hand at Licker and Split playing pool with Red Wing and Githead —"who are wearing the same jean vests with the machete on the back."

Marla blinked and stood back. "Huh," she laughed, "Okay. You've been briefed. And it's your funeral." She turned away.

"Wait, wait, Marla dear!" Mike said as his tattooed arm draped over the dweeb's shoulder. "That's no way to treat a guest. Let's serve him." He turned his burned-out eyes, now flashing red, at the dweeb. "What are you having, mister?"

The dweeb looked at him questioningly. "A beer?"

"A beer!" Mike stood back and nodded enthusiastically at the crowd that had gathered. "Bud Light, I'll bet." Which was met with guffaws and even caused Marla to smile.

"Is that what you're drinking?" The dweeb turned and raised eyebrows at Mike.

"Oh, no, not even! Pabst!" he yelled, and everyone raised arms and bellowed, "Blue Ribbon!" Mike focused on dweeb. "That's a workingman's beer, bud. You a working man?"

"Well, yes."

"Where do you work?"

"In pharmaceuticals."

"Pharmaceuticals!" Mike announced to the crowd, which brought great cheers. "Say, you wouldn't happen to have any of those pharmaceuticals on you right now, would you, bud?"

"Not *on* me." And the dweeb smiled slightly.

Marla felt a stir of concern.

"*In* you, then?" Mike asked. The dweeb nodded. "Well!" Mike gave him a hearty slap on the back. "That explains your bravery! If you want something else, we can accommodate." All round sniggers. "But let's see about that beer. You got money, right? You being a working man and all?"

"Well, not much on me."

"But you have a card, right? I'll bet it's an American Express, Black. Marla, do we take American Express?"

"We do," Marla said.

"It's not, it's a Visa." Dweeb explained.

"Perfect!" Another hearty slap, maybe a bit more intense than the previous one, The dweeb winced. "A round for the house!" Which elicited cheers from the crowd.

"I don't think—"

"A round for the house." Mike, intent on dweeb's face, smile gone, murder eyes blazing.

The dweeb regarded him and turned to the bar, fishing his wallet out of his pants and handing Marla the card. She shook her head and rang it up, and everyone reached over the bar or into the coolers and made off with a beer or two.

SlingBlade, the owner, ran up and down yelling, "Just one, goddammit!" and threatening everyone with his bat, but they all just laughed and pushed him away. Candy and a couple of the other girls, only wearing G-strings, helped distribute until everyone had at least one, maybe two, some with three.

Marla popped one open and placed it in front of the dweeb. "Your beer," she said, making sure to swish the vest and give him an incentive. Not that she was worried about her tip anymore. She was going to add whatever amount she wanted to the card.

"So let's see what we got here," Mike said, seizing the wallet and flipping it open, first extracting about fifty dollars in ones and fives and throwing it over his shoulder. "You guys keep playing eight ball, courtesy of our friend," and he scrutinized the license. "Robert Chantrelle, of Utterson. Hmm!" Mike cocked his head in appreciation. "That's kind of a high-falutin' town over there, Mr. Robert Chantrelle. Bit outside your bailiwick, ain't ya?" He flipped the license to Marla, who caught it deftly and slid it into her jean pocket. She'd make sure the dweeb got his license back, if he survived.

"I needed to get out," Dweeb said.

"Pressures of the job, huh, Robert?" Mike tsked. "Makes you indulge a little product, does it? What exactly was it, anyway?"

"An enhancement."

"Really?" Mike nodded around at the others, his mouth twisted in appreciation. "Like a dick enhancement?"

"No. More involved than that."

"But still, gave you a big old hard-on, didn't it? Made you feel tough. Here you are." Mike stilled, and Marla said a silent prayer. "I mean, you getting an eyeful of the lovely Marla here, and that's just making your dick throb, isn't it?"

Robert blinked at her slowly but said nothing, and Marla felt uneasy. There was something in the dweeb's eyes, something ... predatory.

"Yeah, she makes all our dicks throb." Mike tightened his hold on Robert, the hand sliding down to his hip and then around his neck, a loose chokehold. "But I gotta tell ya, Robert, you're actually making our dicks throb more."

Robert blinked up Mike's arm. "Excuse me?"

"Yeah, Robert, you are." And Mike spun him about so he was facing Crewcut and his big gap-toothed smile, the meth eyes spinning and spinning. "See, my boy Crewcut here," a gesture with the free arm, "likes boys. Or men. Especially cherry men. You're cherry, aincha, Bob?"

"I don't think—"

"You don't think?" Mike sported a look of fake astonishment. "I mean, you either are or not. If you're not sure, Crewcut and Red Wing and Githead," who had stepped away from the game for this new sport, "will take you in the back and confirm, either way."

Split and Licker laughed nastily from the table as Mike wriggled his eyebrows at the dweeb. "Mike," Marla warned, but he winked at her, so this was still just sport. For the moment.

"Yeah, come on, honey, let me make a man outta ya!" said Crewcut, who was in on the game because he hated gays, went out of his way to break them when given the chance, so Marla should have relaxed.

But the dweeb wasn't in on the game, and who knew how this would end?

"C'mon!" Crewcut insisted and grabbed the

dweeb's lapels, and Mike squeezed, and Red Wing reached for the dweeb's head. The dweeb pulled back and slapped both hands on either side of Crewcut's head and squeezed, both sides of the head meeting in the middle of the spine, brains and blood spurting out as though Crewcut's head had exploded. Which it had. Like a squeezed Ding Dong.

"What the fuck!" Mike yelped, real shock in his voice. He pushed away, but the dweeb grabbed his arm and hoisted him straight into the air, straight over his head, and hurled him across the bar and into the pool rack, breaking just about everything there. Mike bounced off it to the floor, leaving an indent of Mike in the wall, reminiscent of an old Bugs Bunny cartoon.

Marla screamed.

Red Wing unsheathed his machete and, yelling bloody murder, swung it hard at the dweeb's head. The dweeb grabbed it out of the air, twisted and doubled the blade back, blood pouring from the deep cut in his hand, which exposed bone, and then grinned at Red Wing as he drove the bent blade right through Wing's throat, blood spraying everywhere.

SlingBlade charged across the room, the bat ready, but the dweeb stopped him mid-charge with a raised palm to his chest. It looked like Sling had run straight into a wall. He gasped and staggered, and the dweeb stepped in and drove his fingers into Sling's chest and pulled out his heart, took a bite, and tossed it over his shoulder, almost hitting Marla, who was too shocked, too terrified, to do anything else but watch.

The smart ones ran. But there aren't a lot of

smart people in a motorcycle gang.

It took about three or four minutes, and when all the screaming and pleadings had finished, all Marla saw were arms and legs, some of them no longer attached to bodies, bodies no longer attached to heads, bodies opened up so various internal organs flopped out, and one guy, Chainlink, even had his legs tied behind his head. Literally.

The sudden quiet as terrifying as the previous screams, the dweeb stood in the middle of it, pools of blood and brains around him and on him, bleeding from a deep gash on his head and the wound Wing had inflicted and, as Marla watched, the wounds closed up and smoothed over as if nothing had ever happened.

"It's a pretty good product, don't you think?" the dweeb said to the air.

"Wh-what?"

"It does what's promised." He turned about and looked at her, his face expressionless. "It accelerates healing while reducing the pain threshold." He held up his previously cut hand and stared at it in wonder. "I didn't believe the guys at first, but when I saw the trial results ..." He shook his head. "Well, I just had to give it a try."

Marla couldn't breathe, the stench of guts and blood choking her, and she backed away slowly as the dweeb continued to examine his hand. Sling had a sawed-off shotgun in his office, and if she could just reach it ...

A pair of hands like vises seized her elbows, and pitched her over the bar, almost landing on her face, but she turned in enough time. A knee pressed on her back like a boulder. "That guy Mike was right about one thing. It does make your dick throb."

It was like a donkey and a bull and a pile driver at the same time, and Marla screamed as she was ripped open, and her pelvis broke, and her hips broke, and she broke. But not before she was flooded with what felt like a gallon of battery acid.

She cried, quiet, shocked, feeling herself pass out. The dweeb stood over here, adjusting his pants. "Sorry about the mess," he said, and she could tell something had gone out of him. Well, no kidding.

His breathing slowed and he blinked slowly, and suddenly turned beet red, like someone coming down from an acid trip. The dweeb staggered a bit, then stood up straight and turned to the door, "I'll see you later, Marla."

You sure will, dweeb, Marla promised, already formulating how many times she was going to shoot this bastard as she kept a hand over the pocket containing his license.

A ROSE BY ANY OTHER NAME

A Rose by Any Other Name

"They're not zombies."

Zeke stared at the forty-or-fifty decayed, shambling, dead-eyed corpses on the other side of the chain link fence, screaming for his blood or brains or guts or whatever they could tear off his body. "Coulda fooled me."

Jericho tsked, slapped another clip into the mini-14, and hosed about twenty of them back so the fence wouldn't collapse. "That's because you have no sense of etymology."

"I don't think they're bugs, Jer." Zeke blasted a couple more with his own Mossberg .12, then jacked another round as the zombies, staggering and confused, pulled themselves together for another assault.

"ET-a-mology, not ENT-a-mology," Jericho said as he eyed a group of near-skeletons ripping at a loose portion of the fence. "Etymology is how a word develops, and I'm telling you those things aren't zombies."

"Well, why don't you tell *them* that?" Zeke blasted a couple of rounds at the fence-tearers.

"A real zombie wouldn't behave the way these things do," Jericho said, studying the warehouse. Still needed to find a way in there. He fired up a cigarette. Zeke would love to pull out a cigar and join him, but that would be too distracting. One good thing about recent events: bad habits were now inconsequential.

"They look real enough." Zeke brought the shotgun down to waist level because the fence was holding. "So why don't you explain why they aren't?"

"Be glad to." Jericho took a long drag, evaluating a possible entrance near the dock. "A real zombie is a slave, raised from the dead to serve his master."

"That's a vampire," Zeke snorted.

Jericho shook his head. "No, it's not. A vampire is a blood-sucking demon. They *will* raise other vampires, but that's mostly accidental. Like spreading AIDS."

"Or whatever caused all this," Zeke gestured with the barrel at the zombies crowding the fence.

"No ... well, you *could* make a vampire analogy based on the epidemiology of the virus or radiation or whatever generated them."

"What?"

"Never mind. Back to the subject." Jericho walked briskly past the loading dock, and Zeke fell in, covering their six as the zombies (yes, Jer, zombies) roared their displeasure and tore anew at the fence. Wasn't going to hold much longer. "A zombie is a deliberate creation. A voodoo priest makes it."

"Makes it what?"

"Makes it a zombie. Keep up, will you?" Jericho made an impatient gesture, and Zeke wasn't sure if he meant the topic or the platform he'd leaped onto.

"So a voodoo guy makes zombies?"

"Yep."

"Yeah?" Zeke thumbed back at the fence. "Why would voodoo guys want to make things like those?"

"They don't. That's the point. That's why 'zombie' is the wrong term." Jericho began pulling on the only un-padlocked door they'd found so far.

"Dude," Zeke expressed his annoyed confusion as he added muscle to Jer's efforts. They got the door partially open, and both of them slipped through, shoving the door back into place. Should hold.

"I'm tellin' you," Jer insisted as he spot-lit the rows of stacked pallets disappearing down the aisle into dusty murk. "Real zombies are just slaves, not cannibals."

"What kind of slaves?" Zeke followed Jer's light, watching for movement, and wishing he had lit that cigar.

"Whatever the voodoo priest wanted. Usually, work in a mine or to kidnap white women."

"Huh?"

Jer's hand wave threw the beam off. "In those old 40s movies."

"Didn't see any of those, Jer."

"Okay," Jericho walked to the end of the first aisle, peering at the labels. "I guess all your zombie lore is based on Romero, right?"

"Well, yeah!" Zeke read the stack opposite. Lima beans. Ugh. "I mean, that guy was dead on. And long before those things started popping out of the ground."

"Hey! Creamed corn!" Jer yelped in pleasure, and they both pulled off the plastic and put one full crate on the floor. "And how does a headshot work against them?"

"Well, it doesn't."

"Right," Jericho began poking at the next pallet. "So how accurate was Romero?"

"It was just movies, Jer."

Jericho laughed, then said, "Bingo!" as he pulled plastic off the second pallet and began stacking crates of water bottles. Better than gold. Zeke abandoned the corn and grabbed one of the bottles, broke off a cap and downed a whole liter of the precious stuff. Jer plopped down next to him with his own bottle.

"Which is the point I'm making," Jer picked up the conversation. "You can't go with some director's take. You have to go with true definitions."

Zeke wiped his mouth. "You can call them dirigibles, for all I care, Jer. Doesn't make them any less dangerous."

"No, you gotta call them what they are."

"They're zombies. Flesh-eating, world-screwing zombies, Jer. That's all there is to it."

"Ach." Jericho shook his head sadly. "That's what happens. You start calling Democrats 'liberals' and homosexuals 'gay', and both words lose their true meaning. Same thing here. Everybody calls them zombies because that's what Romero called 'em, and the only link between them and real zombies is they rose from the dead."

"So what?"

"So what?" Jerry blinked at him. "Listen to yourself. How many people died thinking that whole Romero headshot trope actually worked?"

"Well ... a lot." Yeah. A lot. Including Zeke's first group, shooting and shooting and shooting as an ever-increasing wave of zombies, attracted to the gunshots, overran them; and there was Zeke, hanging from a rafter, watching as the zombies ate his two best friends, his mother, and his girlfriend. Good thing Jer and his pals came along about then, and cut their way through to rescue him.

"You bet 'a lot.' And that's because they were misidentified. See, definitions are important." Jer raised an emphatic finger, then used it to poke some more holes in the plastic.

"Why?"

"Because ... " and Jer probably had a real good answer that would have bored Zeke to death, except a zombie jumped off the top shelf and wrapped its fingers around Jer's throat, cutting his response to "*Urk*!"

"Dammit," Zeke muttered and rolled away, gripped the shotgun and smacked the butt of it against the zombie's head. That drove it back far enough, Zeke was able to blast it in the chest. The zombie flew, rot and offal spraying everywhere, and landed on its back, stunned. Zeke walked over, pulled out his hammer, and spiked the zombie through the knee to the concrete floor. That should hold it.

"You all right?" He stooped next to Jericho, who was massaging his throat and trying to talk. All Zeke could make out was "bastard" and "burn the sonofabitch."

"Did he bite you?" Zeke readied the shotgun.

Jericho violently shook his head and just as violently pointed behind Zeke, no doubt wanting him to douse the zombie in lighter fluid and torch it. Uh uh. Damn things burned like paper, and the last thing Zeke wanted to do was set the warehouse on fire, at least before they'd emptied it. "Now, Jer ... "

Jericho's violent pointing got even more frantic, and he was making "*Urggh*! *Urggh*!" sounds suspiciously like a zombie, or ghost, or whatever, and Zeke warily raised the shotgun but then heard shuffling and turned.

The spiked zombie was still down, of course. Took 'em a while to recover from a gunshot, and even longer to work their way off spikes. But the five other zombies coming up the aisle were definitely a problem.

"Dammit." Zeke started blasting, taking out two with one round (pretty good, pretty good), waited for the smoke to clear to see if any others approached, no, then walked over and commenced spiking. He needed two more spikes and came back to Jer. "Got any extras?"

Jer was standing now but still couldn't talk, and handed over a couple while massaging his throat harder. Based on the sounds he made, these were his last spikes. Zeke went back and finished the job. By that time, the first zombie was pulling at its trapped knee, so Zeke smashed its head into jelly (like that meant anything) and walked back.

"I'm down to two rounds." Zeke held up the shotgun. Jer's eyes blazed in rage, and he pulled harder at his throat while grunting something to the effect of, "I TOLD you to bring more, didn't I?" Yeah, yeah, gimme a break. "We better go." Zeke gestured at the crates.

They found a tarp and piled up the water and creamed corn and dragged it all to the other side of the building. There were forklifts here and there but, after this much time, no way they worked. Jer mini-14'd a couple more zombies that came at them from another aisle, and Zeke cracked them senseless, in lieu of spiking, more proof they really needed to leave. Now.

Zeke yanked up the warehouse door and stepped onto the platform, ready. Clear. Zeke's pickup truck was still there and unbothered. Just hope it starts.

It did. Whew.

They threw the last crate on top, and Zeke tied them down. Didn't want 'em slinging off while they were racing through a zombie horde. "I get what you're saying," Zeke said, since Jer still hadn't recovered his voice. "I guess they are more ghosts than zombies, all coming back from the dead and being all evil and stuff. Wouldn't make very good slaves, either." He chuckled as he tightened the last bungee cord. "But, you know, that's what everyone's calling 'em, so ..." He shrugged and tugged and was satisfied and glanced over at Jer, who was standing, quite motionless, next to the passenger door, looking off to the fence line.

Zeke followed his gaze. Yep, a pack had just appeared around the corner, no doubt attracted by the engine. Please don't conk out, please. And there were growls coming from deep within the warehouse, so the shot zombies were mobile again. "Let's go, partner," Zeke called as he slapped the side of his truck (good ole Ford) and thanked God he didn't latch the big warehouse gate like Jer had told him to do because he figured they might have to make a quick getaway and the gate would now push open with a nudge and not wreck his front end.

Jer hadn't moved. "Dude." Zeke slapped the truck again, louder, "I said 'let's go'." He walked up to give Jer a push.

And that's when he saw the blood dripping off Jericho's hand. "Crap," he leaped back.

Jericho turned and stared at him. Or, sort of stared. His eyes were already turning white, the skin turning green as lines of rot followed the veins and arteries from the bite mark, partially visible under Jer's collar. A tooth fell out as Zeke watched. Didn't take long.

"Crap, crap, crap," Zeke said all the way around the truck. He got in, belted, then rolled down the passenger side window. Jer's lip was curling into a snarl. Didn't take long.

Zeke sighed. Jer had been a good, if annoying, partner. The others would be upset, but the water would ameliorate. Ameliorate. That was a Jericho word.

Zeke raised the shotgun as Jericho took his first shuffling step toward him. "Zombie, ghost, whatever." He fired.

Then drove away.

BANSHEE

Banshee

Ashford had never seen her before, and he'd remember because she was striking, tall and pale, and accented by a ravishing crown of rope-thick black hair that hung well past her waist. Well, he presumed it hung that far; he couldn't actually see her waist. The woman strolled along the far walk, partially obscured by the ground's dip and a retaining wall. All Ashford could see was her head and shoulders, and that magnificent curtain of pure black hair, gliding along as if she floated.

"Lovely," he said softly, surprised when the woman turned and looked at him, right at him, with green, green eyes. How extraordinary, a color combination of ocean, and night sky, and snow. She smiled with teeth of pearls, and Ashford was momentarily confused because surely there was no way she could have heard him at this distance, surely. It was a football field or more to her floating figure, and there were trees and birds and the evening breeze piccolo across brush and branches and, even more, how could he see that extraordinary eye color so clearly?

"Excuse me," Ashford raised a finger in emphasis and lurched forward—all he did these days was lurch—and caught her suddenly raised eyebrow and querying tilt of head so, good, yes, she will take his interest, probably in a laughingly dismissive manner because a woman so striking certainly would have little tolerance for a man clearly past his prime, but too gentle and sophisticated to simply spurn him. That would come after a few minutes, in a kindly manner, but at least he'd have the experience of her. And, perhaps, who knows, more than dismissive interest?

The trees blocked his view and he had to weave to keep her in sight, and, my, this was getting harder to do, wasn't it? He cleared the bordering shrubs and was full on the beach, overlooking it actually, the bank crumbling at point break, and tumbling to the sands that rose to its base and out to the water, misted and sprayed and rolling off the setting sun ... and there was no one there.

Not entirely true; there were beach walkers and hardy sunset surfers and umbrellas here and there, and some ethnic music with the requisite acrobatic dancers showing off to impressed bikini-wearing women; but the pale angel, the gloriously-haired green-eyed wonder, nowhere to be seen.

"Extraordinary," Ashford told the sea.

Ashford's balcony overlooked enough of the sea to make his view lucrative, but it wasn't a million-dollar configuration, just enough to be satisfying. That was an excellent summary of his entire life: one quite satisfying. To think he would end in a somewhat tasteful condominium within sight of the Pacific Ocean, with foregrounds of Spanish tiled roofs leading the eye to the slant of ocean and mountain that canted about forty-five degrees from sky to water on his right, all of it tumbling down a rather tasteful slope to where he could just make out the beach. Nice.

"Summary? Does that mean we're at the end?" he asked the beaded curtain hanging off the balcony, and laughed. Maybe. Such things were under nature's control, but he's not exactly ready for it to end. Got a few adventures left to undertake. Maybe surfing, which at his age would truly be courting disaster, but wouldn't it be cool? Marjorie wouldn't think so. She thought everything he did was of the 'court disaster' type and never cool. For a woman so good in bed, she had a stick-up-the-arse personality. You'd think he'd have learned from her not to select a wife based solely on bedability, but it's what he did. Marjorie first, then Chloe (any woman named Chloe had to be good in bed, it was like a rule or something), then Marjorie again, and then Selinda, and as predicted, now, no one.

Perhaps that should be his next adventure—marry for the fourth time. Wait, is it the third time? Do you count marrying the same woman as separate conjugals or just an extension?

The phone twittered, and Ashford picked it up. "If you marry a woman twice, is it a single marriage with time off for good behavior?"

There was the expected stunned silence on the other end. "Uh," Seymour began, as he always began when responding to one of Ashford's off-the-wall questions, "Dunno, Dad. Why, did you propose to Marjorie again?"

"Tut," Ashford tutted, "call her Mom, not by her name. It's disrespectful."

"She told me to."

"Doesn't mean that you should. And, no, no proposal, we haven't actually spoken in a while."

"Thank God," Seymour breathed, "I sure don't want to go through that again."

Ashford was about to dispute who of the three of them actually went through what the first two times, but Seymour, suspicious, broke in. "Why did you ask that?"

"Why did you call?"

"Question with a question, Dad. You respond to mine first."

"I taught you well. Okay, I saw the next Mrs. Tellerman on the beach yesterday."

"Oh Lord," Seymour gasped, "what's her name, Ingrid or Livia?"

"You're funny. Actually, I think it's Houdini."

The resulting silence begged further explanation, so Ashford obliged. "She disappeared right in front of me."

"Probably aware of your reputation. So the reason I called ... the last contract with the school system is about to run out, so I'll go ahead and do a standard renewal."

"That's fine. You're in charge, do what you think is best."

"Yeah, until you hear about it from someone and then scream, 'why wasn't I consulted!'"—here, Seymour broke into an astoundingly accurate Ashford impersonation—"'It's MY name on the company! MY reputation!'"

"I don't do that."

"Uh huh."

"Okay, well, yeah, because it's true, but you are

in charge and I think that's fine, and did I tell you that she has the most extraordinary green eyes?"

A long sigh from Seymour. "Still on this, huh? Okay, good, means you won't notice when the expiration dates change, and when you call and ask what happened, I will remind you of the green eyes."

"You won't need to. The green eyes will be sitting here next to me."

"Okay. Bye, Dad."

"Bye," and Ashford disconnected with a sense of satisfaction. Seymour was the good one, all Ashford's brains, all of Marjorie's looks. "How could a kid get so lucky?" he asked the balcony.

And saw, on the beach, the pale angel. Looking right at him.

Which was impossible. The beach was a mile away. The balcony had an unviewable angle. The bead curtain obscured all. But her eyes were locked right on his.

"I love you," Ashford said,

She smiled. Those pearls, clear and appreciative, those eyes, warm, and an invitation.

Didn't have to tell him twice.

It took him longer than he wanted, and much of his breath to make it beachside, but he was here, by God, and where is she, my future wife? Ashford scanned the area, peering hard at the bikinis and muscle shirts and umbrellas and gigantic surfer waves, but she wasn't here. She just wasn't. Dammit. Took too long. She got bored and went off with some surfer dude. Shuffling over to a parking lot bench, Ashford slumped heavily and wondered at his hard breathing. My goodness, actual spots before the eyes. Maybe he should think about restarting some kind of exercise regimen because he was going to need all the stamina he could muster when he got the girl into his bed. She looked like a hellion. He smacked his lips in anticipation and breathed deeply. Get it back, man.

You shouldn't be this out of breath.

No, he shouldn't. He frowned at himself. What is this? Is the lifeline that he presumed stretched to infinity farther along than he thought? Intellectually, he knew that was impossible, and the line could cut at any point for arbitrary and often whimsical reasons, but, c'mon, he wasn't THAT old.

Was he?

He contemplated mortality until the spots dissipated and his breath regulated, sat back luxuriously against the bench, and watched the beach antics until they made him chuckle. I'm alright now, I'm alright. He stood, wheeled about, and headed to the path, and looked up at his distant balcony. And stopped cold.

She stood there, framed against his balcony doors, looking at him. Those green eyes, eternal. And pitiless.

"What do you know about the Angel of Death?"

Seymour, although used to Ashford's off-the-wall questions, this one threw him for the proverbial loop. "Uh, what?"

"In all of your mythology and pagan literature studies that I paid for—"

"Comparative Literature, Dad."

"Yeah, whatever, money well spent, I'm sure, did

you come across it?"

"Well, not specifically."

"Why's that?"

Seymour was intrigued enough by this off-the-wall question that he hadn't hung up by now, something that usually occurred the moment Ashford disparaged his choice of studies. "Because there's no course in the syllabus entitled 'Angel of Death, a Perspective.' Or 'The Wit and Wisdom of the Angel of Death.' Or 'Tropes and Meanings of the Angel of Death in Relation to Postmodernism'—"

"Okay."

"'—The Angel of Death as Metaphor in Classical Etruscan Poetry.' 'The Angel Gabriel as Archetype of the Angel of Death and Satan as Envisioned by Milton in an Unpublished Draft of Paradise Found'—"

"Okay, okay."

"'—1950s Sitcoms as Substitute for Angel of Death Fears by Recently Returned WW2 Veterans'—"

"Okay, okay, OKAY!"

Seymour stopped, a restrained chuckle on his end. "I could go on, if you want."

"No, that's fine, I catch your drift."

"Good. So why did you ask me such a bizarre question?"

"Because I saw her. It." Ashford hesitated. "Her."

"Gonna have to explain that one."

"She was standing on my balcony."

"Who was?"

"The Angel of Death."

"Okay. Still need further explanation."

Ashford sighed. "You remember the girl I told

you about, the future Mrs. Tellerman?"

Seymour was a quick study. "That's the girl on your balcony?"

"Yep."

Seymour laughed. "My, my, you do work fast. And already she wants to kill you. Tell her she has to get in line."

"That's not funny."

"Actually, it is. I'd better let Marjorie know, because she's harbored this long-standing fantasy about cutting your balls off. About to get preempted."

"I said this is not funny. I mean, I'm serious ... this is something very strange."

Something in Ashford's tone drove Seymour off the one-liners. "Okay, what's going on?"

"I can't really describe it. This girl, this woman, I mean, we have some kind of connection. But it's at impossible distances. It shouldn't happen."

"What do you mean, 'impossible distances'? Wasn't she in your apartment?"

"Yes, and I was on the beach."

"So, she broke in."

"No, no, ah!" Ashford sputtered his exasperation. "I'm not explaining this right. She couldn't have been in my apartment because she was on the beach first. When I got to the beach, she was on the balcony. There's no way that's possible."

"Maybe she's a track star."

Silence. Ashford couldn't find the words to express his metaphysical dread, that what he encountered was, indeed, The Angel of Death.

"Dad, there's no such thing."

"She's coming for me."

More silence. "Dad, I think you need to go see a doctor."

"Too late for that." Ashford moved to disconnect, but then said, "When they find me, remember this conversation." This time, he did hang up, cutting off Seymour's, "Dad, what are you—"

The sun had set. The witching hour. Wait, isn't that midnight? Ashford checked his watch, and it was only a bit past seven. Let's not wait for midnight, then. He went to bed.

Someone was screaming.

Yanked out of sleep, Ashford bolted upright, gasping in terror and wildly casting about, and what is this? What is this? It took him several terrifying moments to realize it was no dream, it was not happening in his room, and it was midnight.

The witching hour.

Ashford gained control of his breath and leaned forward, re-examining the room to make sure the screamer wasn't within reach. He unclenched his hands and slid out of bed, heart pounding, ready for combat. Moonlight and the breeze streamed through the balcony doors as he satisfied himself the screen was still locked. Slipping carefully to it, he peered one eye around the edge, convinced a green eye would meet his. But no one was on the balcony. Sigh of relief ...

... and a scream rose, a small and expanding crescendo of low flute to screeching, ear-breaking horror. Hands slapped to his ears, Ashford yelped with the pain of it and stumbled back against the bed, falling heavily. Even through his tightly plugged ears, he heard the final notes die away, in sorrow, in tears, and oh my God, someone is mourning and it is soul-shattering. His gasp turned into a sob of sympathy. No one should endure this much grief. No one.

Staggering to his feet, he edged to the balcony again, peered out, and there, way out there, on the edge of the retaining wall, the pale angel. Of death.

Her back to him, that ravishing hair lifted and flowed in the breeze, as alive as she was. Or wasn't. Her arms were straight down the sides of the funeral shroud she wore down to her ankles, illuminated in ivory by the moonlight, and outlining the glorious shape of her ... and how is he seeing this?

She tilted her head back in angle with the moon, and a low tone, at the level of Ashford's bones, sounded from her and scaled in frequency and height up a long, steep mountain of grief as her hands rose in time with the volume of it, until it was that unearthly shriek of pain and sorrow, hands twisted to the moon imploring and crying, waves of the scream pounding up her body and though her arms to the moon itself.

"Oh, God!" Ashford cried: this was mortal anguish, the soul torn in half by the mournings of the Earth. He blindly made for the door, crashing several times into chairs and jamb before he fumbled his way into the hallway, and down the stairs, and stumbled outside, the night wind surrounding him and urging him on. He cracked his toes on the edge of the parking lot and mounted the berm, running barefoot and almost naked, except for his sleep shorts, through the sand and ice plant, to where she was bright and blazing against the far wall, shining through the blocking trees, beacon. The shriek reached a peak, and held, an ululation of pain, and Ashford cried, tears flowing until he reached her.

He panted, hands on his knees, directly behind her, unable to catch his breath to call her, to tell her it was all right, these sorrows, these griefs accumulate until they are anchors on your heart, but it'll be okay, it'll be fine. You just have to give it enough time ...

And the anchors dropped on top of him. Marjorie first, then Chloe, and Marjorie and Selinda, and the things he had done to, and not done, with Seymour, all the roads not taken, the roads he shouldn't have taken, the infinite regrets and mistakes of a life now over. All beyond redemption.

Now over.

Ashford stood, the weights pulling him down to the earth: she turned and faced him, and oh, God, she was so beautiful, so filled and ethereal, the moon and the stars in her hair ... and what's that beyond those eyes, what's that?

A chance?

He took her hand. And was gone.

BY THE LIGHT OF THE SILVERY MOON

By the Light of the Silvery Moon

A tide pulled at Cassandra, like sitting on the beach as waves washed over her feet, then rushed back to the ocean. She went to the window, enticed, beckoned. By what?

It was dark outside, the nightlight reflected her in the window, and she had to admit, not bad. Long, black, luxuriant hair falling down her shoulders Elvira-style, although she didn't have the shock of white hair. Should think about that. She looked thirty, not forty, and could pass for twenty when she wanted to at the bars when she wanted someone thirty. Smooth, high cheekbones, her eyes were green, sometimes orange when she was lit from inside, as she bounced on a 30-year-old who was always stunned the next morning when he, or she, found out how old Cassandra really was.

Creature of the night.

Had to laugh. Where did that first come from? Not Elvira; that was "unpleasant dreams," which had a tease in it. Dracula, right? No, that was "children of the night." Whatever, it was the kind of B-movie schlock she had always enjoyed, and all those vampire women, the brides of Dracula and Count Yorga and, yes, Elvira, were timeless and beautiful, no matter how many centuries old. Elvira still looked good. Perhaps she was a real vampire.

Perhaps I am, too.

She preened a bit and probably could do so for another half hour, but should go to bed because work in the morning and the furniture store wouldn't open itself; customers were important if she was going to make her rent, so she needed to look thirty, even though forty, because that was young enough to attract the wives' husbands and get them to open wallets to buy overpriced and rather uncomfortable side chairs, while also convincing wives that Cassandra was experienced enough to speak confidently about Floyd sofas and no, dear, it fits right in with your Walmart décor, you'll be the envy of your cashier friends. So she had to get some sleep, otherwise the dark circles under her eyes would make her look like a true vampire. Or a zombie.

But the tide ... it pulled, truly pulled, and she frowned and squinted, and maybe she should turn off that light so she could see better ...

... what's that?

A glow down the hill, just above the tree line. What IS that? A fire? A campfire. Someone on the other side of the trees, along the creek, hotdogs and beer, teenagers grabassing—they'd best be careful before they burned the woods down. Gawd, Cassandra, you ARE getting old.

No. Not fire. The moon.

The top of it cleared the trees, bigger than it's supposed to be, which was an illusion, she knew, and orange, not an illusion, like her eyes when passion-lit. She felt something rise within her, and she frowned. It's the moon. I've seen it a thousand, a million, times.

Why am I so drawn?

Perhaps the earlier thought that she was getting old, a thought that intruded more frequently these days. An extra line around her mouth, an ache in her back, a growing reluctance to prowl the bars for those thirty-year-olds. She wasn't foolish enough to think it was avoidable, nor that she should undertake actions to forestall it like surgeries and makeups. No. One must always bow to the inevitable, but one shouldn't expect the inevitable to arrive so early. She still felt years of energy in her. But maybe she was kidding herself.

The moon was timeless. Cassandra was not. Maybe that's why she was drawn.

She stood, expectant, wanting to be assured. The moon will always rise, the Earth will always turn, this is her time, and she can look back on a rather wild and interesting life with some piles of wreckage here and there, a couple of husbands, a sibling who no longer spoke to her, but that was inevitable in a life well-lived, and she had no regrets. Well, some, but they were twinges, ephemeral in the face of a rising moon.

Everything turned out fine. Everything will be fine, the moon said.

She frowned. Why was she relating to the moon?

It's not like she was some kind of stargazer geek, like that kid in high school, what was his name? Oh, yes, Heimie, the blundering, awkward, horn-rimmed glasses held together with tape, who was so in love with her and had asked her out, and she, more amused than anything, had said yes, and he picked her up and drove to the fields where she was about to question what he thought was going to happen—and given his unexpected boldness, may actually happen—when he pulled a telescope out of his trunk, set it up, and said, "Come look." And she did, laughing under her breath the whole time, but it was sweet, it was innocent, not what her usual dates wanted, so she had kissed him when he dropped her off, and never went out with him again. But did not ridicule him to her friends, either.

Was this draw, then, some kind of flashback? A harkening back to a distancing youth?

While she considered that, the orange light turned argent, and the world was bathed in silver: the leaves on the trees glowing with it, the shrubs and the lawn now cast in it, and she held her breath because the pull was stronger. "Come out," a fairy voice whispered, "come see the night in silver." Slowly, she pulled the drapes over, unlocked the French door, and stepped out, barefoot, onto the deck, and she was moonlight, lustrous.

Her hands: she turned them over. No emerging spots on the back of them, no scars from years of work, the batterings that a life well-lived inevitably caused. She was something else now: Diana, the silver huntress riding her chariot, casting the beams down from the heavens. She looked down at her nightgown, billowy and translucent in the ethereal light. She pulled out the Mary medallion she always wore between her breasts because her mother had given it to her—the only reason she wore it—which glowed in the moonlight because, of course, it was made of silver. Like calls to like.

Something called, "Come on. Come out."

She tripped lightly down the deck stairs, laughing at her foolishness and feeling, oddly, like she was twelve. Running through the woods with her cousins and her sibling when they were all still friends, hiding in the woods and making firefly lanterns, and scaring each other: that was magic, wasn't it?

Is this?

No. It's most likely age.

She trotted toward the wood's edge and concluded her tides were turning down and this was a yearning for those younger days: let's play again, let's be foolish again because we don't know when these urges dissipate. Not that she believed she would ever run out of vim and vinegar, as her mom described it, but it would come less and less. So indulge the moment.

Cassandra crossed the wood border and marveled at how easily she moved, no stumbling or cutting her toes on sticks or thorns, as if she were some sylvan being, like the one calling her deeper into the trees. What would she find there? Old men dressed in gray robes stitched with crescent moons and stars, standing in a circle around a stone altar bearing knives, awaiting her? Or fairies skittering about a pond in an eldritch dance, holding out their tiny hands and grinning with their too-sharp teeth? No, nothing like that. Something nice.

She broke through the woods and into the small clearing that bordered the next set of trees sloping to the creek, where she stopped because of the moon. There, posted above the trees, pulsing. "Oh my," she whispered as the druid light flooded the area with a thousand years of forgotten gods and heroes, the world altered to its other sense, the things not seen. "Look at this," she whispered and stepped clear of the branches and into the middle, held out her arms bathed in silver, in a cloak of time before time. She laughed and threw her head back, and exulted in the nether light. "Feeling pagan, are we?" she chuckled.

A rustling behind her.

She gasped and turned—it must be some raccoon or fox running through the woods. At least she hoped it was, because she was flimsily dressed in a wooded glade, with anyone who could help well out of earshot, and what are you thinking coming into the woods alone at night? I am thinking that something called me. That the moon is my friend.

It isn't.

Whatever launched from the woods was so fast. All she could see was a blur of claws and teeth and red eyes, the snarling clearer in her ears than whatever other details she made out. She screamed once.

When she woke, it was noon, the sun high above and pitiless, and she had to be dead. Had to be. But dead people don't feel this bad, do they, as if they'd been hit by a truck? She sat up, groaning against the bruises and what had to be deep cuts because of the way her back and breasts screamed at her; she lifted her hands, covered with blood. "Oh no," she whispered. "I'm bleeding. Probably to death."

Shuddering, she pulled her arms in and her legs up to brace and turned on her side: there was a naked man next to her. Her breath stopped because her attacker must not be finished and any moment now he'll stir and, oh, she hurt so much ... could she scream, could she? But the man didn't move, just lay there, staring at her with half-open milky eyes, not breathing. Covered with blood. Hers? She couldn't tell, but in the sunlight, something gleamed in his mouth; she blinked and focused and, what? The silver chain from her medallion. Hanging over his lips.

She was in the hospital for two weeks. Yes, deep cuts, the one on her neck should have been fatal, the one running down her stomach should have disemboweled her, but it must be that she fought back enough, or stepped back sufficiently, to prevent either consequence. At least the cops thought so. "When he bit your throat, he must have swallowed the medal. Killed him." The detective shook his head. "It's weird. Must have had some kind of allergy because it burned him."

"Burned?"

"Uhm hm. Do you clean it with any kind of acid wash?"

"Well, no, just, you know, rinse it."

"Hmm. Must have been a severe allergy, then."

"Who was he?"

"We don't know. No ID. We didn't find a car or any clothes. We think he's been living in the woods. Eating rabbits and other animals."

"But I've lived here for years, and I've never seen anyone out there."

"No accounting for crazy people." The detective gave her a sympathetic look. "You're lucky, very lucky. Probably shouldn't go out in the woods by yourself."

Another week, and sufficiently healed, she could go home; her boss said, "Take your time," and she did, shutting the French door curtains tight and staying in the bedroom, flinching at every noise. No one called. She didn't really have any friends.

Almost a month later, she felt restless. I can't just stay in the bedroom, she thought, I have to get out. So she took a shower, careful of the still sore wounds, and decided she'd wear her hair differently from now on, so she could pretend to be someone else. She pulled her tresses up and out, and the scar on her neck looked different. She peered at it. The way the cuts came together: a star. A five-pointed star.

Something hot ran through her frame, a course of fire and urgency, and she dropped the brush and almost fell back against the wall. Something throbbed, hard and merciless, in her chest; she had to get out of here, just get out. She was choking. She was strangling. One motion of her fingernails and she tore the dressing gown away from her. She ran, so lightly and sure, to the door, her feet gripping and launching her right through the door, practically ripping it in half, and she leaped onto the deck, growling low and murderously, and there, there!

The moon, high and silver, filling her with the blood lust.

She howled once, exultant.

THERE'S SOMETHING
WRONG WITH
WILFRED

There's Something Wrong with Wilfred

Lucinda had lived next to Wilfred her whole life and suffered for it. "There's your boyfriend!"—the hateful singsong of that godawful Claire, head cheerleader and head jerk, pointing down the hall at Wilfred, shuffling along. "He's NOT my boyfriend!" hissed between clenched teeth for the umpteenth one hundred millionth time.

Which brought Claire and her cadre into a semicircle around Lucinda, trapping her against the locker. "Do you sneak through his window? Does he sneak through yours? Be real easy with those legs of his."

At which point Lucinda, books held to her chest, wondered if socking Claire in the mouth was worth the five-day suspension. Of course it was. Seeing Claire's perfect little nose flattened against her perfectly sculpted face, spewing blood all over her perfectly highlighted blonde hair, would be a savored memory over the five days. But then, Mom. And Dad. And Principal Futzen. Oh lordy.

"Does he even have a dick?" Claire, smirky, head cocked, and her cadre, all perfect teeth and coifs, all giggled and echoed the question in alternating parrot voices of higher and higher frequencies.

Lucinda could not help herself. "Not as big as yours."

When it all ended, Lucinda had gotten as good as she gave, but bloodying the cheerleaders was tantamount to peeing on the Constitution; she was tried, convicted, and sentenced to the five days with a follow-up call to Mom and Dad. Oh lordy. She stalked out of the office with Principal Futzen's irritating effeminate voice, more so than Lucinda's, following her, "We don't tolerate this kind of behavior, student!"

"Student." He was too woke to call her 'young lady' or use pronouns like 'her' or 'him' or 'them.' She snorted as she stepped into the hallway and ran right into Wilfred.

"Thank you," he murmured, goon-like, hovering with his not-quite-here stance, hunched and looking off, not at her, in the way he not-looked at everything.

And this was too much. "You know, if you didn't walk around like such a goon, people would leave you alone." And she flounced, actually flounced, around him and out of the door for the walk home. But not before she saw his face fall into itself.

You butthole.

Herself, she meant, not Wilfred; although, look at the guy. Just look at him. Those legs, too long for his body, supporting a neck too spindly to do anything much more than hold up his wobbly head, which was sallow and collapsed; he had a blue eye and a brown eye and hair cut like one of those old Beatles, a round mouth always partially open with teeth in crooked rows like a lamprey. No wonder he invited scorn and jeers. Dude, you should do something with yourself, dress better, not those highwater jeans and dad-button shirts, maybe compensate with cool clothes for what you obviously missed in looks.

You butthole.

Her, again, not Wilfred. Because everyone had harassed and bullied Wilfred ever since Lucinda could remember, and she had always felt sorry for him, but could not come to his defense without being accused of girlfriendhood or dweebness. That one year, fifth to sixth grade, when the goon had suddenly shot up to six feet or more with those wretched, unworkable legs that had made the basketball coach ... what was his name? Oh yeah, Captain Leather. Well, that's what they called him because he looked like an old purse ... despair of using this sudden God-given center. And Lucinda swore he had two brown eyes, and then that blue one showed up. What a goon. Ick.

So are you.

She kept up the flouncing all the way to her bedroom, flopped on the bed, and felt like such a heel. A turd. A goon. She rolled over to face the window and Wilfred's house next door, dark to the point it almost blended into the background, which was all trees and bushes and overhang, as if the place was slowly being absorbed into a jungle. All shades down. No car in the driveway. A goon's house.

Mom and Dad came home at their irregular times and regularly screamed at her about behavior, and it simply didn't matter whether Claire had thrown the first punch—you don't hit back—and she wondered aloud what she was supposed to do then, allow herself to be murdered? Naturally, she was not displaying the proper attitude. Naturally, because Claire and her squad were untouchables, the offspring of richer and better people than Lucinda, and she should know her place. Well, they didn't say that, but Lucinda felt it was implied, and the upshot, here she was, sun setting, confined to her bedroom so she might reflect on her behavior.

My behavior was justified.

How 'bout the way you talked to Wilfred?

Oh lordy.

She opened the window and slipped onto the back lawn, her favorite way of avoiding parental inquiry, down the hedge, which gave her cover, and did something she had never ever done: walked to Wilfred's front door.

All these years, never been here. No one had. Wilfred put people off. Wilfred was too weird. Wilfred was the loneliest person on Earth, sitting in the very back of classrooms, enduring spitballs and trippings, never, ever saying anything. The education establishment had despaired of him, and written him off as a place filler. As had Lucinda. Bad enough that proximity meant she endured years of 'Wilfred's girlfriend!' accusations; she had never done anything to lend evidence to that by doing anything such as talking to him, or walking up to his house and knocking on his door. In all these years.

Now she felt even worse.

The car was in the driveway, so Wilfred's Dad was home, a furtive man who slipped from house to car with the stance of an escaped felon, short and humped and bald, with little glasses that occasionally flashed at her on the occasion she observed his arrival or departure. Dad and Mom did not like him. "Could do something with that yard," Dad groused. "Killed his wife years ago," Mom whispered, although there was no evidence for that, Lucinda knew, because she had googled it.

There was a Ring. Great. So, not only was she verifying neighborhood rumors of girlfriend status, but leaving evidence of it. She hesitated—a knock on the door was more circumspect—so she did. Three seconds was long enough to wait and, hey, she tried but it didn't work out, sorry 'bout that, and turned to slip back home when the door opened. Wilfred's Dad stood there, blinking at her. "Lucinda," he said.

Which was quite startling. "How do you know my name?" she demanded, not even a 'hello' because this was too weird.

The man shrugged. "I know everyone in the neighborhood. Come in." The screen door opened, and a hand on her shoulder pulled her inside, a kind of kidnapping, and she wondered for a moment if that was the case. One shaded lamp, providing all the illumination in the dimly lit living room, which was probably for the best because her first impression was of dingy and shabby. Beige walls and ceiling, both of which could have stood a de-cobwebbing; brown couches and side chairs that sagged in the middle, and needed replacing; some kind of light-absorbing rug that would benefit from vacuuming. And Wilfred's Dad, who could really stand a makeover.

Look at this guy. Too short for a man, with

Danny Devito hair, except it was gray, eyes that bulged at her from behind way-too-magnifying glasses, and wet-looking lips that seemed on the verge of drooling. Instant creepies. "Nice of you to visit," he said in a squeaky voice, but she detected a note of sarcasm in it.

Best to get this over with as fast as possible. "Is Wilfred here?"

"He's ... resting. Have you come about what happened in school today?"

Again, startled. "How did you ..." But if he knew all the neighbors without anyone knowing him, then he probably knew everything else about the town, too. "Yes. I wanted to apologize to him."

"For?"

His head canted; he was short enough that his straightest stance actually made him look up at her. She fidgeted. "It's something between Wilfred and me. Can he come down?"

"I'm afraid not," said with a little glow in his eye that caused a chill, "Wilfred has a very delicate condition that requires frequent treatments."

"Oh." Hmm. Maybe that explained some things. "What kind of condition?"

"It's a regenerative one." And then nothing. Like that explained anything.

"Okay, well, can you tell him I apologize for being a little short with him this afternoon? I didn't mean to be," and she turned to get the heck out of there as fast as she could.

"He likes you, you know."

She turned again, a desperate feeling crawling its way up her throat. Oh no. Wilfred's Dad noticed that and chuckled appreciatively, "Not 'like' like. As a friend."

Relief on one hand, but, huh? "We've never really done anything together."

"But you are the only person who hasn't bothered him."

Oh my, what a small criterion for being pals. Wilfred must be desperate; Wilfred must be desperately lonely.

Dad nodded thoughtfully and said, "Why don't you come over for dinner tomorrow evening?"

Which was about the last thing on Earth she wanted to do. That must have shown because Dad held up his hands in placation. "I understand if you don't. But it would be very appreciated. Besides, Wilfred is an excellent cook."

"Wilfred?" She couldn't keep the surprise out of her voice.

"Yes. He has the brain of a French chef. You might be pleasantly surprised," said in response to her obvious surprise.

Well, that would certainly be different, wouldn't it? "Okay," she said.

"Excellent!" Dad beamed. "Let's say eightish? It'll be dark enough by then, so you won't be seen." Pause. "No need to slip out of the window," and he gave her a wry smile as he propelled her back down the hall and out of the door. She stood on the porch as the light went out and wondered what had just happened.

And what was that smell? A whiff of something as the door closed. Ammonia?

Maybe the house was cleaner than it looked.

First day of house arrest, and it went pleasantly, Lucinda blowing off the punishment essay about why she should not use violence to deal with conflict. It is to laugh. Slapping Claire around had been quite satisfying, and that recommended a greater use of violence against buttholes. She did not blow off cleaning the house from top to bottom as a placation of her parents, who were still muttering about her suspension, and how that would look to colleges, and again, it is to laugh, because Lucinda had no intention of going to college. She was going to California. But best to waylay inquiries in that direction and appear the dutiful daughter.

Which almost killed her, even through dinner, which she picked at with a remorseful expression on her face that she hoped would stave off commentary, but no such luck. "You need to finish your plate."

No, Mom, I need to leave sufficient room for what promises to be a very unusual dinner that may or may not kill me, and may or may not be satisfying, and if that is the case, then I will eat when I get back. But best not to convey these plans. "I'm still upset."

"As you should be," spoken triumphantly and she was excused to go to her room to finish her essay and, fat chance.

Sunset and dusk came up, and it was drifting past eight, but it didn't feel safe until Mom had made one last check of Lucinda sitting dutifully at her desk, with a look of concentration on her work. Mom nodded her approval and was gone, and so was Lucinda.

"Sorry," she said as Wilfred's Dad let her in.

A breezy wave of hand. "Think nothing of it. Fashionably late is a statement of fashion," and she followed him toward the living room and brought up short. That smell ... that wonderfully savory smell. "What is that?" she marveled.

Dad smiled. "Come see," He led her into the kitchen, and Lucinda strolled through the gates of heaven. Steam rose from the pots and pans on the stove, and she saw what looked like a stew in the middle one, rich and dark and smelling of wine, with a pot of what looked like pale-peachy soup next to it, and another pan of what looked like steaming vegetables on the other side. Opposite, on a granite countertop, a gigantic bowl filled with the best-looking salad Lucinda ever saw, various greens and reds, and what was that, stuffed grape leaves? Next to that, a loaf of bread, perfectly brown, steaming as if it had just come out of the oven.

Hunched against the far cabinets, wearing a red checked apron and clutching an oversized spoon and fork, Wilfred. Head down as usual, lamprey mouth open, trying to disappear into himself, but she saw the look on his face and knew what she had to do. "My God," she breathed in the kitchen perfume, "this is WONDERFUL!"

And like a float thrown to a drowning man, a pat on the head of an abandoned puppy, the flush of joy across Wilfred's sallow, fallen face, and he slowly looked up and at her directly for probably the first time in his life, and whispered, "Thank you," his voice like a rasp against stone. And for the first time in a very long time, Lucinda felt good about herself.

French bistro salad and lobster bisque first, then beef bourguignonne and ratatouille and asparagus and potatoes, with varying types of creams and seasonings, all served with a French wine that was, in Lucinda's case, a major violation of state law, but which Wilfred's dad assured her was customary in Europe. "Besides, I won't tell," and he toasted her with a twinkle.

Just Lucinda and Dad, mostly, because Wilfred spent his time hustling between the kitchen and the table, each dish served with eyes averted. Then he stood anxiously in the doorway, bobbing uncertainly on his spider legs until Lucinda tasted it and then, "Oh, wow!" and stared at him in amazement. He smiled, ducked his head, and went back for something else. Dad encouraged more wine on her and urged the tastings and re-tastings, and it was so obvious he was terribly proud of Wilfred, and Wilfred terribly anxious to please.

How terrible.

The guilt avalanched over Lucinda at dessert, *mille-feuille*, and her third glass of wine, and she wondered how much of that was alcohol induced or genuine. She knew she was a happy drunk, based on the two or three previous and furtive incidents, so the guilt was all her. "I really don't know what to say," she said, when Wilfred, finally, slid as unobtrusively and quietly as possible into the chair farthest from her.

"Say what you think," Dad encouraged, a tip of the wine glass at her.

Okay. Do this. "Wilfred." She turned and looked at him, straight and square up. "You are a genius. A full-blown, unmitigated, frickin' genius," which was, as far as Lucinda was concerned, the highest of praises.

Wilfred ducked his head into hands held in prayer, jamming his lips against the thumbs, and giggled; a strange, almost hyena-sounding thing that should have startled her, but his eyes got so big and glowy that she thought he was going to cry. Dad smiled and nodded at her.

"And I apologize," she said, "I really do. I have treated you like crap all this time. Everyone has." A resolve filled her. "I'm going to tell everyone what a genius you are."

"I'd rather you did not do that," Dad said, gently.

"What?" She was genuinely surprised. "Why? He's such a talent." Said with a gesture at Wilfred that made him bite his thumbs in pleasure.

"Yes, he is, but he also, well, has a delicacy that too much attention could adversely affect."

"What?"

Dad sighed and looked at Wilfred with a mixture of affection and concern. "He has an immune disorder that can be aggravated by many circumstances, including a lot of attention. It's why he's standoffish. Why he acts like, I think as you put it, a goon."

Floored her, that did. Look of incredulity at Wilfred. "You do that? On purpose?"

"At my direction," Dad said.

She stared at him. "Well, that's just wrong. He could have had a lot more fun and a lot more friends if he hadn't ..." She almost said 'acted like a goon all the time' but refrained, " ... kept himself apart from everyone. We'd all have seen what a great guy he is."

Okay, so maybe she was putting it on a little thick, but parents could be such buttholes, and this weird Dad was being a real big one, keeping his son all repressed and stilted because he might get sick. She doubted whether a goon like Wilfred could have done much better socially than he already had, but at least no one would think he was retarded. Just goofy looking, which oftentimes had its own cachet, if played right.

"Oh?" Dad looked at her mildly, "You would have come over to the house, then?"

Lucinda liked to think of herself as more of a rebel than a follower of the various crowds, and she wasn't exactly a member in good standing with the various cliques—except for her own crowd of social rejects and outcasts—but there was a limit to the actual practice of rebellion. She could drive her parents up to a certain point of grounding, with privileges taken away, but not to the point of military school. And she could see and sympathize with Wilfred's predicament, but the merciless razzing and insults she would have endured as Wilfred's friend was a bridge too far. "No," she said softly.

"Ah," Dad nodded with satisfaction and a small smile, proving himself right as all parents did. She looked at him with resentment and then glanced at Wilfred, who had collapsed into his hands, his eyes downcast, and she swore he was going to cry.

"But I'd like to." As soon as she said it, she could have kicked herself in the head, but look at Wilfred, his eyes up and shining, looking so hopeful. She steeled herself and smiled at him.

"Really?" Dad said it in a way showing he half-believed her, but then scrutinized his suddenly smiling son and nodded. "Would that be all right, Wilfred?"

"Yes." A rasp of a voice, barely discernible. But imbued with happiness.

"Well, fine." Dad regarded her. "Say tomorrow night, then?"

"Uh ..." Oh Lordy, what have you done to yourself, Lucinda? "Sure. For dinner?" An upside.

"Well, yes, but that will be this," a gesture at the table, "warmed up. Trust me, though, it tastes better the next day. No, tomorrow you will see something quite different. I think you'll be pleased. We'll clean up," and he nodded at the door, and she was on the front porch, the door firmly locked behind her by a firmly ushering Dad.

She stood on the porch, not sure what had happened. Tomorrow night, something quite different?

Please don't let it be *Dungeons & Dragons*.

It wasn't.

It was an aria.

Wilfred stood, mostly self-conscious, in front of drapes in the living room that Lucinda swore was an actual theater curtain, lamps on the floor shining up and making him look like a ghoul. That had been disturbing, as was the old and shabby couch Lucinda sat upon, unsure how long it had been since it was cleaned. Dad sat in an equally shabby overstuffed chair that had the stuffing leaking out of the sides, but looked comfortable all the same, nodding quietly along to a gramophone—

an actual, honest-to-God wind-up gramophone—with a scratchy record spinning on it, and Wilfred sang.

Sang? Is that the word you use for heavenly choirs?

And 'choirs' in the plural, because Wilfred was singing two voices at once, which had to be impossible, and Lucinda suspected there was a microphone or some other device on him, but she couldn't detect it. So, how? No one can do this. No one. Except Wilfred.

Lucinda knew nothing of opera, but she was pretty sure this was called the Butterfly Song or something because it was the only opera she recognized besides the William Tell Overture, which the school orchestra manfully played at assembly year after year. She remembered it because it was the most beautiful opera song she had ever heard.

Wilfred turned it into a religion.

Well, as close to a religious experience as Lucinda had achieved so far, except for the time Rohan Wills had fingered her to the point of what she thought must be an orgasm, but she couldn't really tell. This felt a lot like that, er, sounded a lot like what that felt like.

It was an aria for two women, sopranos, and Wilfred couldn't sing soprano because he was a guy. Right? She'd heard guys sing like girls before, but it was strained, and mostly falsetto. She didn't think a guy could do this, unless he was what they called a *castrato*. Was that Wilfred? Well, it would certainly explain a lot.

When he was done, Wilfred simply stood there, eyes downcast, a flush to his face, clearly pleased.

He should be.

"That's," she breathed, "impossible."

Wilfred looked startled, but Dad merely laughed. "You'd think, yet, there it was."

"I mean, that was unbelievable and wonderful," here, Wilfred clasped his hands together, smiling, "but it just can't be done." She looked over at Dad. "Did you do something?"

Instant darkening of the face and alarm. "What do you mean?"

She made a helpless gesture at Wilfred. "Something electronic. Some kind of illusion." Geez, what did you think I meant?

Dad relaxed. "Oh, I see. But no, this is all Wilfred."

"But ... how?" Repeat of the helpless gesture. "Wilfred, how did you do that?"

"I just can." With his head still down.

"He has the lungs and throat of a diva," Dad said.

Which was an odd way of putting it, and she shook her head admiringly. "Wilfred, that is a talent so big and important you have to let others hear it."

He started like a frightened rabbit, eyes so big, she clearly saw the differing colors. "No," he rasped.

"But, Wilfred," she persisted, "you're so good! You should let the other kids hear you." Left unsaid: maybe they won't pick on you so much, call you a goon. Then again, they'd treat him like an idiot savant, so how was that an improvement?

"No," Wilfred breathed, visibly shaking now, and she frowned. What was wrong with this guy?

"Wilfred," she insisted, "if I had a voice like yours, I'd want everyone to hear it." True. Instead of being a picked-on nobody, she'd be a picked-on somebody.

"NO!" Wilfred fell back against the makeshift stage, his arms raised, warding her in terror, his eyes about to pop out of his head ... and then they popped out of his head.

"What the FUCK?" she shrieked as she came up and almost off the back of the couch, watching with a combination of revulsion and fascination as Wilfred went rigid, like a board, and then shook like a paint can mixer, the eyes flopping around on his face.

"Wilfred!" Dad came out of his chair and wrapped his son in a bear hug, trying to hold him up. He looked over his shoulder. "Help me!"

There was no way in heaven or Earth that Lucinda was going to touch Floppy Eyes Boy, and she shrank against the cushion. "Now!" Dad ordered, and there was such command in his voice that Lucinda found herself grasping Wilfred's shoulders before she knew enough to be revolted.

Somehow, they dragged him up the stairs and into a small room at the end of the hallway, where she almost dropped him when she cleared the sill because this was a hospital room: beeping equipment, IVs and medical curtains and what looked like a stainless-steel oven and machines with green screens and squiggly lines. Dad hauled Wilfred across to a hospital bed and picked him up, dropped him gently on it, and, boy, Dad must be really strong. Wilfred was groaning now, head lolling from side to side as his eyes flew around like nunchucks.

"Hold him," Dad ordered, and again, here she

was bracing icky Wilfred against the hospital mattress without thinking about it, her bile rising as she watched the two little eggs attached to Wilfred's head by bloody cords stare at her. Dad pulled up Wilfred's sleeve and had an IV in it, and Wilfred stopped shaking and relaxed into the bed with a sigh, and Dad popped the eyes back into Wilfred's head.

Lucinda stepped back. "What's. Going. On?"

"Sorry." Dad leaned back from the bed, scrubbing at his hands with a cloth he pulled from a container located on the wall. "Wilfred suffers from a condition."

"I'll say!" Lucinda stared at the now calm Wilfred. "Is he blind now?" Which would be just one more anvil dropped on Wilfred's head.

"No." Dad finished cleaning up. "These eyes will still function. But probably not for long."

"Oh, man." She shook her head, hearing that anvil whistle down. "What's this condition?"

Dad was bent over Wilfred now, checking him with a stethoscope while monitoring the green displays and their wiggling lines. "It's an auto-immune problem. His body regards his organs as cancers."

"What?" Lucinda was round-eyed. "You mean, he's rejecting his own liver and things?"

"Sort of."

"Oh my God," she said. "That's terrible. How long has that been going on?"

"How long have we lived next door to you?"

"Oh my," she said again, this time with more feeling. "All this time. Can you fix it?"

What a stupid question, Lucinda; just look at

the boy, obviously dying. Dad let out a large sigh and leaned over Wilfred. "I've tried," he whispered.

"So are you like a doctor of some kind?"

"Of some kind. And I think I've done a pretty good job with Wilfred, considering. But I think it's getting to be too much."

"What is?"

"The transplants," he toned.

Lucinda blinked. "Wilfred has had organ transplants?"

Dad nodded. "Yes. Several. Repeatedly. Of just about everything." A gesture at Wilfred's head. "Including his eyes."

Lucinda furrowed her brow. "Wait. Those aren't his eyes?"

Dad pointed down the bed. "And those aren't his legs."

Wilfred, coming into school one week with that tremendous growth spurt ... Lucinda backed away, waving her hand in denial. "That's not possible."

"Usually," Dad leaned over, checking Wilfred's eyes.

"But ... what ... how?" Lucinda was making helpless gestures.

"I have a certain skill set," Dad deadpanned, "I know that's a popular phrase these days, but it's true."

Lucinda *twa*'d. "Nobody can do that."

"Most nobodies," Dad acknowledged, "but I can." And he looked at her mildly, and, as bizarre as all this was, she knew it was true. She threw her hands up. "How can you do this?"

He apparently misinterpreted her meaning because he said, "I use ... donations. Unfortunately,

I can't get them through the transplant network. Takes too long."

Huh? Lucinda was thoroughly confused. "How else do you get transplants, then?"

"I have an agreement with certain funeral homes."

Lucinda goggled at him, uncomprehending, and then at Wilfred. "Oh my God," she breathed.

"And I think that's the problem. Those ... donations ... are long dead by the time I can get them attached. Wilfred has done well with them all this time, but not so much anymore. His rejection rate is increasing." He gestured at the eyes. "I think I need to try something from someone living."

Was he saying what she thought he was saying? The way he looked at her ... "You can't mean me," and she backed toward the door, ready to flee through the nearest exit, door or window, didn't matter.

But he held up a hand. "No, Lucinda, not you. You are Wilfred's friend. And we're both hoping you can help us with this."

"Help you? You want me to help you murder people?"

"*Tsk.*" Dad waved his fingers in dismissal. "Not murder. Recycling. From someone who doesn't deserve it, to someone who does." He made a dramatic gesture at Wilfred.

"And why does he deserve it more than the original owners?"

"You heard him sing. You know how gentle he is. What an extraordinary soul he possesses. One of these days, he will lead the human race to a higher level. Or at least should have the chance to do so.

Don't you think?"

Lucinda regarded him with all the consideration one gives a crazy person. But, then, look at Wilfred lying there. So helpless. So lonely. So mistreated his whole life, and he wasn't such a bad guy. He could be brought along, he had potential. At that moment, Wilfred opened his eyes, and Lucinda could see how loose they were, how hard to control.

"Please," Wilfred whispered. And her heart broke.

"What do you want me to do?" she said.

"Nothing too involved. Just lead me to the right people. You must know someone very healthy, quite robust and strong, who doesn't deserve what they have, don't you?"

Lucinda considered. "I can think of a few."

Wilfred had very nice eyes now. Blue. Matched. The kind that would make a cheerleader jealous. Lucinda saluted him at their weekly dinner, and he blushed but was pretty happy about it, and Dad gave her a list.

At a memorial service held in the school gym afterwards, Lucinda stood in the line that queued up to Wex, Claire's occasional boyfriend, to express sympathies and hang in there, man, they'll find her. Or at least part of her. Ha. And Lucinda glanced with amusement over at Wilfred, standing self-consciously at the other end. "Wex," she said, pressing his arm in sympathy. Measuring the muscles. "I'm so sorry." Pause. "Do you have a really strong heart?"

"Well, yeah, I do," Wex said with a puzzled look,

and Lucinda patted his other arm and walked away while giving a surreptitious thumbs up to Wilfred.

TRANSPARENCY

Transparency

Lily moved easily through crowds, having developed in sixth grade the ability to dodge and weave in a way that attracted no attention. She blended into the wakes of the more popular and boisterous, all eyes on them with little noticing of her, the thin shadow behind and beside. Teachers forgot about her, only aware when they graded her perfect papers, frowned and checked her name a couple of times, scrutinized grade books, scanned the room, and found her. Oh, that girl. They wondered how they had overlooked such a good student, but then one of the boisterous or popular would do something to draw their attention.

Not that she wasn't noticed. The crueler of her classmates always saw her, always knocked books out of her hands, or tripped her, or commented on her dress and hair and pointy glasses, and wound themselves up to do more damage and then just ... stopped. Perhaps she blurred into the lockers as she stooped to retrieve papers, or a nearby boisterous or popular started something more attention-getting and, like that, she was free. She found it a much better strategy than fighting back or crying. Blending into a neutral background kept the torment to a minimum.

Lily had stopped attracting notice at home much

earlier, around four or five years old. Up until then, the daily needs of a child required the ministrations of an adult, but her parents discovered that Lily was enamored of picture books and would scoot over to a heater vent with a pile of them and sit there, fascinated. Mother checked on her frequently, but as months passed, she checked less and less. Mom could safely get a lot of housework done in the three or four hours between checks. Mom even got a job. Her father came home and spotted her there, nodded in approval, and then went to do Dad things with the more boisterous of her siblings, who were more popular than her.

Not that she was neglected; she was just otherwise occupied. She attended dinner and sports and television-watching, played games with her three brothers and four sisters, and never gave anyone trouble, or a reason to see her. Her name was a bit hazy to both parents because they rarely had to use it. She didn't grieve about the unfairness of it. It made her happy.

She taught herself to read from the picture books, already at third-grade level when she started kindergarten; her teachers amazed and relieved because she didn't require a lot of support, which gave them more time for the boisterous. They just pointed her toward the room's bookshelves, filled to overspilling with things ranging from picture books to novels way too hard for her. For the moment.

Lily discovered joy.

The stories and the pictures and the clean white pages made her swoon; internally, of course, she would never make a scene. She stood quietly beside the shelves and sorted through them, a blank expression on her face that belied her internal excitement, and almost hysterical response, to Beezus and the Happy Hollisters and Nancy Drew. These were the people she wanted to know. These were her friends, and the life for which she yearned.

Her real life wasn't bad—far from it. Anyone would envy her. She was well fed and provisioned and dressed and thought highly of whenever anyone remembered enough to do so. But she had no illusions about herself; she walked out of step, was the last person thought of, and did not have the urge to be anything else. Because she had other worlds better than this one.

Attractive, diminutive, and thin-featured, with green eyes and blondish straw hair, she had male regard, boyfriends at the appropriate periods in her life, some of them among the most popular and boisterous who accidentally noticed her weaving through the hallways, and went, "Man, who's that?"

She didn't spurn them, actually liked them, and lost her virginity to one who saw her for longer than the others. It became part of her identity to be known as X's girlfriend or Z's woman; she attended the best parties, noticed and approved until she blended into woodwork and smoke-filled rooms, and the memory of her became hazy. It suited her to be a minion in the various crowds, a part of them but not actually, and while her name invoked a nod and a smile, no one could tell a story about her. There was sparkling anonymity in a crowd.

In the same way, Lily made it through college, which was just high school writ larger. There was a sorority in which she made dutiful contributions, and even had a fiancé for almost a year, earning her the regard of others without any of them remembering her name, even the fiancé, who was probably the only one in her life who suspected something else was going on with her. If he had not been distracted by a more boisterous and popular senior, and with Lily's tacit approval, withdrew his troth, then he may have figured out what that was:

Camouflage.

She was the fawn in the high grass, the spots and colors blending and allowing her to remain unbothered as she pursued her true passion, those books. Those other lives. Before anyone became worried about her, she'd subtly direct them to her appearances on campus, the regard of professors, and the completion of a business degree as proof of her normality. Distracted, they never noticed her many absences, even from her job as a document editor and technical writer, who always produced enough to avoid censure. She could slip in and out of her office with nothing more than a tilted head in acknowledgment, through the lobby and onto the sidewalks, weaving in and out of crowds, toward her favorite second-hand book stores, unnoticed.

Until she wasn't.

"You must really like it here."

Startled, Lily stepped back and almost upended a stack of books in one of the back aisles, looking wildly about for the source of the voice. A hand reached out and steadied her from behind the stack—which was even more disconcerting—and this time, she turned too fast and the books upended. She gasped. Damaged books were a crime.

"Oh, sorry, so sorry! I didn't mean to startle you!" yelped the owner of the voice, a wan young man with a black hair cowlick that threatened world domination, a pair of unfashionable black glasses that failed to hide the laser blue eyes, and an earnest expression of true concern. He stooped to help her recover the books, and both of them sorted and restacked for a few moments, until they examined covers and blurbs, read a few pages, and passed them back and forth, wordlessly. The bookstore owner, Pat, peered around the corner to see what the noise was about, nodded, and went back to his register.

That was Lily's first date with Sam.

He was another internal, not as capable of disappearing as she was, but he had a knack for world negotiation, and thereby kept himself in better contact with society. At first, she thought he was one of the boisterous or popular, but soon realized he knew how to *be* with them, but not *of* them; an excellent strategy. It was almost similar to her ability to appear as a popular's appendage. But Sam's meant he didn't need to be attached to gain entry; he just simply showed up. Lily met his coworkers at the graphics design company, where he installed and fixed proprietary software, and even met Sam's parents when it became a given that the two of them were a couple. She supposed they were. They had sex at Sam's little apartment, which was over another used-books store, and, after, they were there searching the stacks, happy.

They were not drawn to the same things. Lily focused on story, regardless of genre; if there was a life lived from the first page to the end, she read it, even if it was a terrifying life, or sad. Sam, though, was attracted to possibilities, and a lot of his thumbings-through involved old medieval texts and religious writings of the metaphysical kind. "I'm trying to find out who we are," he explained.

"Who?" Lily presumed he referred to humanity, but he shook his head and grinned, "You and me."

"What?"

"We're different," and he smiled mysteriously as they sat cross-legged and naked, knee-to-knee, before his latest pile of newly bought books.

"What do you mean?" Her manner suggested she was alarmed, but she wasn't; she was secretly pleased. She knew they were different.

"Here," he said and pulled out a particularly large leather-bound volume with huge spindles across the front, and even a lock and key, the pages gilt-edged and heavy-looking. "Is that parchment?" she asked in some wonder.

"It is. It's really old. Got it for five dollars from Pat." He shook his head. "He had no idea what it was."

Lily wasn't sure about that because Pat was quite savvy. Maybe he had no use for it or had other reasons. "When did you get it?"

"Last week. I was coming home from your apartment and saw Pat was still open, stopped in, and there it was."

"Why didn't you tell me this before?"

"I'm telling you now. Because I know what it is, now."

Lily scrutinized the heavy, dark, other-worldly tome. "What is it?" she asked. His answer would determine whether she would be angry that he hadn't told her right away, or be impressed with his find.

His smile had an almost devilish twist to it. "A grimoire."

"A spell book?" Said with the incredulity she reserved for such nonsense, a grimoire figuring in some of the stories she cherished, but as a prop or a plot device, not as an actual object. That was foolish.

"Yes!" he said eagerly, almost reverently. "And it's got a lot of alchemy and chemistry and astrology in it. I swear it's bound in human skin."

"What?" She recoiled, at least, as far as the book stack behind her allowed.

"I'll bet this is one of Paracelsus's books." And he stroked the cover lovingly.

"Who?"

"Alchemist. Not important, but this,"—he quickly opened the book to a page—"is ..." and he read aloud:

"'Those of you who are nothing,
The ones who walk beside,
Traverse a world corrupting
Safe, in grace you hide.'"

Sam flourished the page at her. Lily scrutinized its magnificent coloring and rubrics and marginalia, and even one prominent illustration in gold and silver that showed a transparent person standing in front of a tree in an attitude of prayer. The page had what she thought was uncial script, but she was not versed enough to tell from what period and, besides, it was in Latin. "I don't read Latin," she said.

"Neither do I." Devil grin.

Suspicious that he was having her on, because

he did have a modicum of twisted humor, she asked, “What makes you think this is about us?”

“You kidding? It’s perfectly us.”

To which she agreed, and they spent the rest of the evening looking through the book at its magnificent illustrations, *oohed* and *aahed* over the colors so bright and clear after what should have been 400 years or so. She speculated it was actually a modern reproduction, although there was no evidence of that, with what looked like recipes and illustrations of fluid-dripping beakers, and handwritten notes in a cramped Latin here and there that Sam could not read. Lily, then, convinced he was having her on about the poem, delicious in its way, left it alone. They stayed up past midnight and made love, and Lily slept over.

In the morning, Sam was gone. She was a light sleeper and should have heard him get up and go to work, but maybe this was one of those mornings when tiredness had overwhelmed her natural alarm system. And her sense of time. She was late. C’mon, c’mon, let’s go, don’t worry about a shower and all that silliness, just go. But not before she looked over Sam’s bookshelves, selecting a few for her own use, and left him a note that she had done so. She went to work.

No one greeted her when she walked through the door, which was good because she was still wearing the clothes from yesterday, and that should have elicited at least a raised eyebrow from an office mate or two, but no. She smiled to herself with a criminal sense of having gotten away with something. She sat at her desk and thumbed through some manuals before getting started, just to see which needed dumbing down so humans understood them, when Applegate, her section head, walked into her cubicle, frowning. "I wonder where she is now?" he muttered.

"Who?" Lily asked. He was probably looking for Marion, who had an even worse habit of disappearing than Lily. At least Lily left with things done; Marion vanished in the middle of projects. Applegate frowned and cocked his head, as if listening for something, looked straight at her, then looked about again and left, muttering.

Lily giggled and scrutinized a few more pages and figured this was a good time for coffee, so she slipped up the aisle to the break room, and there stood Marion, working a Keurig and laughing over her shoulder at Thompson, the big flirt. "Applegate's looking for you," Lily said.

Marion and Thompson ignored her, still intent on their budding office romance. Lily tsked and moved past them to the real coffee and poured herself a cup, plotting a mild payback. When she turned about, both Marion and Thompson stood, open-mouthed, bug-eyed, staring at her. "What?" she asked.

"Did you see that?" Thompson asked.

"See what?" Lily replied.

"Yeah, that was weird!" Marion laughed. "That cup just disappeared!"

Huh? Lily looked about: all the cups, save the one she had collected, were still there. "What are you talking about?"

"Yeah," Marion laughed, "like my lunch sometimes. I think Lily's taking it."

Lily's jaw dropped. Accusing her, right here?

Was this some kind of joke?

"Nah," Thompson waved that off. "She's too nice to do something like that."

Well, thank you, Sir Galahad, but I don't need you to defend me, and she took a step toward Marion, prepared for a discussion.

"You gotta watch the quiet ones," Marion chuckled, and the two of them left.

"What's wrong with you?" Lily called, but they didn't respond, and she wondered what kind of gag this was. Somebody had come up with an office game, and it appeared it was at her expense.

She rinsed the cup and headed back to the cubicle, which was filled with other people: Marion and Thompson and Applegate and the neighboring cubicle denizen, Lea. "... no answer and no one's seen her," Applegate was finishing up.

"Seen who?" Lily asked. Everyone appeared to be here.

"She's at her boyfriend's." Marion dismissed the whole subject and poked Thompson in the ribs, and Lily realized they were talking about her.

"Okay, ha ha, funny joke, so can we now get back to work?" Lily said with the proper amount of exasperation directed at what was really not a very funny prank. She wondered if she should go to HR and glanced at her monitor opposite, which was dark. And saw Applegate and Thompson and Marion and Lea flitting around, but not her. She should be right there, but no. Sind, in the opposite cubicle, leaned in to take a look at all the happenings, frowning and about to shush them all. Sind was there in the monitor with his disapproving face, but shouldn't have been because she blocked the view. But there he was. It was as though she was transparent.

Like one who walks beside.

She gasped, and rushed to the bathroom, right to the mirror, but there was no one there. She waved at herself and shouted, and Swanson, the HR lady, came out of a stall and stood next to her, washing her hands and humming. Lily said, "Can you see me?" No response.

Lily tapped her shoulder. Swanson brushed it, and muttered, "Flies," and left.

She went outside and dodged pedestrians while looking into display windows as she ran past, and no, no reflection. Almost killed by a taxi when she rushed across the intersection to Sam's and rang and rang his apartment and shouted, and passersby glanced and frowned at the bell. "Must be broke," they said and kept going. Finally, the buzzer sounded, and she rushed up the stairs and into his open door, and he was not there.

But he had to be. Who else let her in?

"Sam?" she called, but there was no response ... except for the sound of fluttering book leaves. She stepped around the corner and there was the grimoire in the middle of his bed, open, and there was the page, the one with the poem ...

Sam's parents cleaned out his apartment after a couple of months, and a few weeks later, Lily's parents did the same to hers, weeping the entire time about their missing girl. Lily sat quietly in the corner, smiling sadly, because no, Mom, I am not missing. I am living. Quite well.

In Pat's store, in fact, sleeping all day and then prowling the aisles, eating food left in the refrigerator, or walking across the street to the Thai restaurant and lifting a delivery order—which always freaked them out—and then curling up in an overstuffed chair and reading all night, trying to put things back where they were before Pat opened in the morning, but not always succeeding. Pat and his staff were certain they had ghosts. They were almost right.

Every night she checked to see if Sam had left a note, because he was here, too. Somewhere. Occasionally, she found a badly scrawled one in a book she was about to read, but it was illegible, which was fine.

The ones who walk beside walk alone.

IF I HAD KNOWN YOU THEN

If I Had Known You Then

Bradford saw the girl slipping through the trees and knew immediately she was a ghost. Nothing that ethereal and beautiful could be human. Elf, maybe, fairy of some sort, but Bradford didn't believe in elves or fairies; that's kid stuff, but ghosts seemed possible. Not as intelligent spirits with purpose, of course, but as a remnant, a recording, say, of an event so intense, so emotional, that it left an impression of itself, and replayed when the conditions were right. Like this: a cold autumn day, wet with passed rain and the promise of a later frost, the sun cloud-obscured, but enough wind tossed the clouds eerily across the sky, silhouetting the taller trees with a misty background. So whatever had happened to impress the ghost's image on the woods had happened under these conditions. Need to find the traumatizing event.

"Did anything happen on my property?" Bradford asked the librarian/historian who lorded over the archives and files of the local historical society, which also served as the only thing approximating a library in this little Adirondack town.

Mrs. Palfrey looked at him owlishly, because eyes magnified behind 1950s glasses, and white hair plastered on either side of her face, made her owlish. “And which property is that?” Bradford pointed it out on the huge plat map, old and yellowed, and looking very much like it had been printed a hundred years ago, hanging on one wall.

“Ah, you have the old McKenzie place, do you not?”

“Uh.” Bradford pulled away from the map. “I ... guess. I never heard it referred to by that name. The realtor called it the Woods Walk.” Which had decided the purchase for Bradford because such a charmingly named place appealed to his long-established aesthetic. Woods Walk. A place of sylvan solitude. Contemplation. Meditation. But maybe it referred to a restless spirit stalking the grounds. If so, then he wasn’t the first one to notice the beautiful girl, and there should be lore. Perhaps about the McKenzies?

“Woods Walk? Oh, yes, that’s it, that’s the original McKenzie homestead. Not that there are any McKenzies left, goodness no.” A hand placed to the heart. “They’ve passed out of this area, although there are some relatives still about, in-laws and such.” Said primly and expertly. Then she frowned in deep thought. “There’s nothing that I know of, offhand. The McKenzies were original to the area, farmers and mechanics, but nothing colorful, not like bank robbers or moonshiners,” and she gave Bradford a jovial elbow, which was less than prim and made him smile, and she smiled back.

Maybe there’s a little devilry in the owl.

“Occasionally, there’re stories of ghostlights in the woods and stirrings and a sense of something wrong.” But Mrs. Palfrey had long dismissed those things as just tales carried by the less-educated townsfolk who attributed curses and Indian burial grounds to anything slightly odd. She suggested they take a look in the archives, and no, it was no bother because she had nothing else to do; given that Bradford was the only person in the place, he concluded this was so more often than not.

Together they struck through piles of rather well-maintained newssheets, dating to a time in the 1800s, when the little town of Newfield, New York, had its own paper.

Bradford was amusing himself with advertisements of patent medicines like Smartweed and Belladonna Plasters—hmm, smartweed, whatever could THAT be?—when Mrs. Palfrey cleared her throat. "This might be something."

He read over her shoulder a funeral announcement expressing condolences and sorrow, services to be held on an October day in 1883 for the lovely middle daughter of the McKenzie family, Elice, who passed of melancholia some days before.

"That meant she committed suicide," Mrs. Palfrey toned and blinked owl eyes sorrowfully. Bradford tsked in response. "My, that's tragic. Is there anything else?"

"No. I'm afraid not. There wouldn't be, of course, to spare the family's feelings and such. I may have a birth announcement for the girl in an earlier edition, but unless she did something interesting like won a school prize or was arrested as a moonshiner," a twinkle of the owlish eye, "there'd be no more about her."

"Well, that's sad," Bradford concluded, and then pursed lips. "What was the weather like that day?"

Mrs. Palfrey consulted other portions of the

newssheet and said it was a lovely day for the funeral, bright and somewhat cold, but not enough to repel mourners.

"No," Bradford said, "on the day she succumbed. To melancholia." Further consultation of earlier sheets found it was a cold day, misty and cloudy with a touch of wind. Confirmation, as far as Bradford was concerned. "And where is she buried?"

Mrs. Palfrey pointed out a side window. "I'm guessing in the Presbyterian cemetery. There's lots of McKenzies in there." She blinked owlishly, which is how she always blinked. "If I may be nosy, why did you ask all this?"

"You'll think I'm crazy."

"Try me."

Bradford hesitated, wondering how soon his tale would spread through the village, labeling that outsider who took the old McKenzie place as a crackpot, but, well, he'd never been one to worry about the opinion of others. "I think I saw her."

Mrs. Palfrey's lips pressed firm, and she placed a sympathetic hand on his forearm. "You probably did."

It took Bradford a good two hours to locate Elice's gravestone, the weathered condition of most of the markers, the haphazard placing of family plots, and the lack of a central directory, making the search difficult. All that time Mrs. Palfrey's story stayed with him: the McKenzies had begun a slow decline and die-out about 100 years ago, which was well after Elice's burial, but started with members of the family who were still living when she took her life, which was interesting because subsequent owners of the lovely two-story farmhouse and the lovely woods attached to it, became uneasy after some months and sold to new owners and left town. No one reported an actual apparition, though. Until Bradford.

"I don't know what I saw." Bradford defended himself.

But Mrs. Palfrey was convinced. "Oh, yes, you saw her. It's the only thing that makes sense."

Which, of course, made no sense, unless Mrs. Palfrey also subscribed to the replay theory of ghost appearance. Had to be it, because she didn't strike Bradford as one given to supernatural beliefs, rather the type who sought rational explanations, and if there had long been tales of oddness in those woods, and now a newcomer reported a phantom, well. There are more things in Heaven and Earth ...

So, Elice, are you the ghost?

The stone was so eroded that Bradford had to trace its letters, those that remained above ground level, with his fingers, a difficult exercise, until finally: *Elice Mariane McKenzie, Our Beloved and Missed Daughter. Still Dancing.*

Bradford wondered about old restrictions regarding suicides buried in consecrated ground, but maybe that was too medieval, even for the late 1800s. Besides, the tragedy of it overrode any qualms, and here she was, still dancing. Which, in itself, seemed a progressive thing to say, at least for the times. The McKenzies wanted everyone to know their daughter danced. There was, in that, a peal of grief greater than any statement of how much she was missed.

Bradford felt a pang in his heart, the missing of something he had missed. He had spent his life solitary; a decision, not circumstance. Bradford had a huge world to see and had realized early on that the encumbrance of family diluted that chance. So he had stood on Asian shores, walked Russian ridges, and peered down Peruvian mountains, the effort and expense required to do so taking most of his resources. And time. He had made his fortunes time and again, and lost them in the same periods, and while he didn't mind that, a family couldn't bear such instability.

He'd had women. Quite a few. But the women who circulated through a world like his were of the same bent; attachment was encumbrance, professions of true love interfered, and even when such a profession was made, it was with the understanding of its impermanence. Of those women, there were two or three he considered his one true love during the time they were, and he had no doubt they still remembered him the same way. The one or two still alive, that is.

So he had no reference for a lost child, but he had plenty for lost chances. Her parents had lost the joy of seeing her dance. Elice had lost the joy that others loved. "Elice," he whispered, "why?"

The sun dimmed, and a colder breeze slipped through the stones, caressed his cheek and stood by. He swore he heard a piano playing.

The weather changed, and there were no more replays. The clouds dissipated, as did the mists, and the cold set in, the real cold, and Bradford huddled in warm rooms, surprised at how much it now affected him. He once strolled mountaintops in blizzards and hiked frozen lakes in Siberia, but this little nothing of a winter, at least in comparison, drove him fireside. "What further proof do you need?" he chuckled over his aging. He'd never believed he was immune from it like some of his colleagues, who also thought themselves invincible, and, well, no, they weren't. And he was well aware of all the clichéd symptoms, but to experience it was still a shock. No one believes it will happen to them.

He built decent fires from the decent wood pile left in the woodshed, three or four winters' worth, and he supposed he had the McKenzies to thank for that, because some of the logs appeared to be as old as the family name, which was silly because such logs would be nothing but termite dust after all this time. The shed itself and the *idea* of the pile, then, thank you, McKenzies. And for properly constructed fireplaces, supplemented by more modern inserts and blowers, giving him the ambiance of the country squire in winter, book on afghan-covered lap, illuminated by firelight, tumbler of whiskey on the side table. Just needed the cigar, but Bradford had never indulged, had no taste for it.

All he lacked was company.

Perhaps he should get a dog. Given the tableau, a cat would fit better. But taking care of pets was a bother, and Bradford wasn't sure he had the skill or patience. Which didn't apply to cats. From the rumors, it appeared they took care of themselves.

More bothersome was that the solitude bothered him. He'd sought it as a lifestyle before, but now ... "Further proof of aging," he murmured. When full of vim and vigor, the solitary life was a badge of honor, an aphrodisiac because there was a certain type of woman who was offended by it and took it as her mission to correct the situation. Bradford had taken advantage of them and was not ashamed of it; they didn't read the tea leaves. And none of that type ranked in his 'one true love' category, because who he and they were guaranteed the eventual separation.

But now ...

He stirred restlessly, peeved at the creeping sense of loneliness settling around his stomach. Was it an actual need, related to growing decrepitude and the necessity of having someone take care of him? No, he had enough money to ensure the services of a nurse, should it come to that. This was something else, something a touch frightening ...

That he was wrong. That he had been wrong his entire life.

There is a life well-lived, and then there is a life well-lived uselessly, and Bradford feared his affirmation of the best life he could have lived was flawed, that it was the best life lived by a selfish person. One who ignored obligations. Bradford did not believe people were here for a purpose, whether to please a god or a social order, but the absence of some contribution did raise questions about one's worth. He might say that the things he did expanded the conscience and served as an inspiration, but he had no evidence of this. If there was some bearded benevolent Father waiting on a throne to hear his story, Bradford doubted he could make a case for himself other than, "I had a good time." If all the tropes about that Father were true, then Bradford was going to spend quite a long time frying.

He wondered whether Elice was frying. Suicides were supposed to go straight to the fires, but Bradford didn't think it was that cut and dried. There had to be mitigating circumstances, especially if the suicide was a dancer. God must love dancing. After all, King David danced, and he was God's pal.

Maybe he should ask her.

He blinked at the thought and turned to the French doors behind him that accessed the outdoor patio and gave a view of the woods, but no one stood there, no ethereal girl of beauty. Of course not; it was a bright and sunny day, albeit cold. He'd have to wait for the replay conditions to manifest her. 'Course, since she was a mere movie snippet, there was little chance she would respond to his voice. Too bad. He'd really like to talk to her.

He'd really like to talk to anyone.

Irritated, Bradford downed the tumbler, swept out of the chair, and headed into the kitchen because a liverwurst sandwich was the best cure for the creeping angst, and he made a good one, mustard and all. He swept back into the library in a better mood.

Elice stood in front of the fireplace looking at him. Looking right at him. “This can’t be real,” he whispered.

She tilted her head as if she heard him, and a small elf smile twitched her lips, and my God, she’s lovely. A sepia print, but Bradford knew she had golden hair the color of summer wheat, blue eyes, the skies of autumn, and she wore a white dress that looked like a dancer’s, her arms straight out, and she pirouetted across the room and through the French doors, where she faded into the sunlight. Bradford dropped the sandwich and was out the doors with the speed of a younger man, a caress on his cheek and a whisper in his ear. He stepped toward the woods and saw something misty wind its way through the trees and dappled sunlight.

He heard piano music.

“Tell me about the odd things in the woods.”

Mrs. Palfrey blinked, owlishly of course, and frowned as if she hadn’t heard him correctly. “What?”

“You said people had reported odd things in the woods. What are they?”

“I ... uh,” she was flustered by the question and became more owlish in her scrutiny. “I don’t know of anything specific. I mean, no one has ever seen anything. You're the only one who has."

"And you said it was her. How do you know it is?"

"Well, ah!" A throwing of hands in exasperation. "If there were such a thing as ghosts, then it would have to be her because she's the only tragic figure associated with those woods."

"Umm." Bradford got it. "So a logic exercise. If a, then b."

"Precisely," said with great satisfaction and emphasis.

"But you, personally, don't believe in ghosts."

"No." Said with wistfulness, and she looked away at far distances, and Bradford wondered what tragic figure she saw. "I wish I could. But I have no evidence. I've seen nothing. Heard nothing."

"Heard?"

"Well, eh, yes. Some of the stories say they heard music in the woods."

Bradford sat back. "Piano music." He whispered it.

"Yes." She regarded him cautiously.

Bradford nodded. "I've heard it." He held up two fingers. "Twice." Hand back down. "And I've seen her." Fingers back up. "Twice." He cocked his head. "What does this mean?"

"I ... don't know."

"I'm not crazy."

"I don't think you are. I don't." That last added as an assurance Bradford found suspicious. "I'm sure you saw something. I just can't help you with what."

Bradford sighed and moved back against the chair, one of those old wooden ones with decorative spokes as a backrest that 19th century people thought comfortable. Maybe it built character or something. He looked at her and knew he had to salvage something of his reputation. “I used to think it was ... replay. Just physics. The function of pressure, temperature, and emotion, which simply triggered an effect, in the same way you drop a needle on the same spot on an album and elicit the same sound.” He examined her to see if she was following, and she was. “But yesterday, it didn’t replay. It ... responded. She responded. She danced across the room.”

“Danced?” Mrs. Palfrey tilted a wary head.

“Yes.”

The faraway look in her eyes again. “Some of the stories say the leaves dance.”

“What?”

“In the woods. Without a wind.” There was now a disturbed light outlining the faraway look.

“I found her grave.”

“You did?”

“Yes. Have you?”

“No, I ... I’ve never looked. Never even knew about her until you came in. Besides, I go to other places in the cemetery.” And she was gone again.

“It’s an old stone. Hard to read. But it says, she dances.” He waited. “Still.”

They sat for a few minutes, Mrs. Palfrey far away.

“I have to go,” Bradford said, and did.

The sun had drifted and was somewhere, but Bradford didn't know where and did not care. Its beams sliced through the trees, all of them dust-laden, all of them embracing the trees and brush, lighting them like a fairy landscape, shadow then light and not real, a different country. The sky was clear above the forest, the parts of it he could see speared by the ever-taller trees growing ever higher until he felt he was shrinking. Diminishing.

He strolled with no noise, despite the leaf carpet, the house somewhere behind him, but it didn't matter because he would not go that way again. The light was warm, the air cold, and he reveled in its contrasts, watching the trees stir and reach and bend ever so slightly, in benediction.

There was a lane. Bradford didn't know if it was a road remnant or simply the fall of ground and leaf, but it ran straight and true through the woods to a distance, the trees and sky and covered forest floor converging in that pleasing illusion of a single point, and his feet turned that way. It was clear and undisturbed, and Bradford knew he walked in another world, leaving his behind.

That's fine. He'd done everything with it he could.

There was a light at the end of the lane, and he walked toward it, but it grew no closer. He understood that; it was important to create the distance, to become absorbed in these woods, to be a later whisper among travelers who would look over their shoulders and wonder what that was.

He heard music.

He turned and watched as leaves stirred off the floor and meshed and flowed into a column, windborne, swaying from side to side, gathering more of their cousins into a waltz across the sunbeams and the coolness and the cloud cover, and the mist rose, and she pirouetted toe and ankle out of the center, hand held out.

Bradford took it.

EXCALIBUR

Excalibur

Drew and Dell went to their Dad's funeral. They had no reason to; neither of them had spoken to the old man in years. But Dad's wife, Louise, called Drew and downright pleaded because no other close relative intended to go, which should have been a clue to her. But Drew liked Louise, Dad's fifth or sixth or whatever, and, of all of Dad's wives (including Dell's mother), Louise was the feistiest and friendliest. Drew's mother should have been in the running, but she was never a wife, just an affair. So he'd called Dell. "It's for Louise," Drew said, and Dell replied, "Louise? Yeah, she's all right." And both decided then and there to go, Drew from New York, Dell from California, which was the main reason they had not physically seen each other in a while. Distance. Time. Money.

Scar tissue.

Drew got there first and drove to the house, where Louise met him on the front porch, wise enough to give him a friendly hug without any display of grief. She knew by now grief was uncalled for. Relief, though, was appropriate, and Dell accepted her diabetes tea and snickerdoodles and everything left unsaid, the burdens lifted. One does not speak ill of the dead, so best not to speak at all. Louise regaled him with tales of other relatives

Drew barely knew or did not know and, frankly, cared little for, but it was better than reviewing Dad's life, which was a criminal documentary. Dell got there three or four hours later, and Drew hugged him with genuine affection because the two of them genuinely liked each other. Soldiers in a foxhole.

They went out, finding a dive bar on a side street, and toasted each other and their mothers and their sisters and other assorted long-dead or disappeared associates, and saved the last and best toast for Dad himself: "May he burn in hell," Dell said.

"May his malign influence and genetic material disappear from all existence," Drew replied, and they clinked glasses.

"You're basically asking for both of us to die," Dell pointed out.

"It does sound like that, doesn't it? But we are diluted versions of the Great Bastard,"—their pet name for Dad—"so we get a pass."

"Here's to dilution," and they clinked glasses again.

The funeral was well attended by Louise's relatives, because it was a southern thing to support the widow, regardless of whether they liked Dad or not. Also by a few strange women who had probably convinced themselves they loved, or were loved, by Dad, and had come out to see. Amazing.

"Maybe they think Dad has left them something in his will," Dell speculated.

"Yes, the vast Becker fortune," and they both giggled, which was inappropriate at a funeral, even the Great Bastard's, and they got severe looks. The open casket was a southern thing, too. Drew and Dell exchanged looks and dutifully went up to take a look, more as confirmation than anything, although Drew expected Dad to rise up and start drinking everyone's blood.

"Doesn't look bad," Dell said.

"No. Dead is good on him," and they sat and then attended the reception afterward to support Louise, ate and drank more diabetes-inducing foods and liquids, and listened to the diabetes-inducing expressions of sorrow Louise had to endure. Drew and Louise periodically exchanged 'oh brother' looks, to Dell's amusement.

Then it was time for the reading of the will.

"We're in it?" Drew was surprised.

"Yes," Louise responded. "Of all his kids, you're the only two."

Of course. None of the sisters would be in it, nor any of the other unacknowledged. Drew got a pass because he had served in the Army, which was Dad's alma mater. "So that's why you wanted us to come."

"Yes."

"Hmm. So, what, he's left us a dollar each and a paragraph or two of vituperation?"

She gave him a half smile. "The words you use. But I don't know what's in the will."

Double hmm.

Actually, it wasn't that bad. Louise got the vast Becker fortune—chuckle—Drew and Dell given their pick of Dad's possessions, which was like a Dollar General collection, but there were some decent fishing rods that Drew claimed, while Dell said, "You don't mind if I take the guns?"

"I thought you couldn't have guns in California."

"Which is why I want them."

Drew waved assent and took one more look around the rummage sale that was Dad's garage, and noted a tarp in the far corner. Probably some tackle boxes. Drew grabbed a corner, pulled, and launched centuries' worth of dust into the air and, by the time he hacked his lungs clear and the dust settled, Dell had made his way over. "Waddyaknow," he said.

"Yes, waddyaknow," Drew confirmed. Dad's old Army trunk, from dubya dubya two, when Dad drove a tank in Patton's Third Army, a time in his life of which he said very little, and had never, in living memory, allowed anyone to open the trunk. Drew had earned one of his many Dad-hidings from an attempt to do just that. No danger of hidings, now. Unless Dad rose from the grave, something Drew considered a possibility. "Shall we?"

Dell had picked up quite a few mechanical skills in his life and had the old Master padlock, which was probably as old as the trunk, open in a matter of seconds. Interesting stuff inside: Dad's file folder containing his military records ... "And his court martials," Dell speculated ... numerous photographs of Dad on a tank or standing next to a tank, and group shots of other tankers and buildings on fire ... and rows and rows of bodies ... hmm. Wonder if that may have affected Dad's psyche? ... and, of course, lots of foreign-looking women, probably English and French and Dutch and German, a sordid memory from every country he had been. Buttons, badges, an odd medal or two. "You want this stuff?" Dell asked.

"The pictures are interesting."

They agreed to split the contents evenly and laid what they wanted into two different piles. Drew was about to close the trunk when he noticed something in the far corner. A box of some kind. He pulled it out. "Wonder what this is."

"Probably his deal with the devil," Dell said as he examined Division patches.

Drew fished at the corner, snagged the box, and pulled it up. Odd thing, wooden, very old wood at that, a little off-square and covered with lines like someone had scratched it with a knife. It had an odd smell, camphor mixed with cedar, and Drew guessed there were mothballs in the trunk somewhere. It had some weight to it, and Drew looked for a catch, but there was nothing obvious. "What do you think this is?"

Dell looked over and shrugged. "A medal."

"You think Dad won a medal?"

"For shirking or drunkenness, sure."

Drew considered and then shook the box. There was definitely something inside, but he was damned if he could figure out how to get to it. He tossed the box to Dell. "See if you can open it."

Drew examined. "Looks like someone tried to get it open with a knife ... wait." Furrowing his brow, he twisted the box in and out of the attic light. "These are words."

"Oh, yeah?" Drew leaned forward. "What's it say?"

Dell pulled out his cell phone and played the flashlight across it for a moment. "Dunno. Looks like Latin."

"Really?" Drew followed Dell's beam and,

waddyaknow, it did look like Latin. Thing must be really old for all the letters to be that worn down. "Can you read it?"

Dell looked at him. "Can you?"

"Nah. Never took Latin."

"Well, then, let's Google it."

They did. Or, they tried. For some odd reason they couldn't quite get the letters in the camera frame, and when they entered them manually, the result was gibberish.

"This is not working," Dell announced unnecessarily.

"No kidding, Sherlock." Drew stared at the box. "So what do you think this is? And don't tell me, 'medal.'"

Dell shook his head slowly. "No idea. Something valuable, though. Dad probably stole it while raping his way through Europe. Do you want it?"

"Do you?"

"Ah," Dell nodded sagely, "so you, too, think this might be the fabled Becker fortune."

"Vast Becker fortune."

"That, too. So probably best to keep this between us?"

"I think that's wise."

"After all, who of all the various half- and quarter-siblings we share the world with deserves it more?"

"That's good thinking," Drew said, "so what are we going to do?"

"I don't think it's a good idea to break it open," Dell shook the box. "There's something obviously inside, but the box, itself, may be real valuable. So we need someone who can read Latin." Dell raised a querying eyebrow.

"Don't know anyone, off hand."

"Me either. But isn't there a fairly decent university near here?"

"There is," Drew acknowledged. "One of our removed cousins or unacknowledgeds got a Physical Fitness degree from it. Which I found out today, from Louise."

"How fortuitous, although that doesn't bode well for an antiquities department."

"Well, we are out in the country, but you never know."

"So we should call them."

"Yes, we should." Emphasis on the 'we.'

They held each other's gaze for a moment, and then Drew snapped a photo of the box in Dell's hand, and then they switched, Dell taking Drew's. In case of future litigation.

Surprisingly, there was an antiquities department or, more accurately, an ancient history section of the History Department, and a Professor Harold Hill—which immediately launched Drew and Dell into songs about trouble in River City—who said he read Latin and, yes, he'd be interested in seeing the artifact on Tuesday at three. Which added a couple of days more to both Drew and Dell's planned stay, but could turn out to be worth it. After all, this was a treasure hunt.

Respective wives did not understand, immediately suspicious of their claim of extra time with the family, both wives well aware of what kind of family the brothers came from; "It must be other women!" something that always made Drew laugh because, oh please, one irrational, demanding, nagging and judgmental person in his life was quite enough. But let them think that, as long as they didn't press too hard.

Drew and Dell almost burst out laughing when they walked into Professor Hill's office because, my God, it was Robert Preston, complete with bow tie.

"Yes, yes," Hill eyed them balefully, "I know, and I've heard it a thousand times, trouble in River City, Marion the librarian, so come up with something unique." And he sat back in a rickety wooden chair, expectant.

The brothers exchanged looks. "Shipoopie?" Dell ventured.

Hill nodded. "Okay, that'll do." He held out a hand, fingers wiggling. "Let's see it."

It was Drew's turn to safeguard the box, and he fished it out of his jacket pocket. Hill narrowed his eyes as he hefted it. "Hmm."

"What?"

"This looks like a Druid Box."

Drew raised eyebrows. "Which is ...?"

"What it sounds like. Something a druid keeps his favorite spells and herbs in. In some games, anyway."

"Wait," Dell shifted. "What? A game? This is from a game?"

"Probably."

"What game?"

"Some *Dungeons & Dragons* thing. One of the players probably made it for his character."

Dell and Drew looked at each other, speechless, then burst into laughter. "Dad, a gamer." Drew wiped his eyes. “Too much.”

Hill blinked at them both. “I don’t have the reference.”

“We found this in Dad’s old Army trunk and, believe me, he was no gamer.”

“Not fun games, anyway,” Drew added, and Hill looked at him.

“I see. What made you think it was Latin?”

“The writing on it.”

Hill peered at the box. “That’s not Latin. That’s Ogham.”

Dell tilted his head. “Viking runes?”

Drew scored Dell a point for knowing what Ogham was, as Hill mused. “More Irish, but the Irish were Vikings, so yeah. Celtic, more accurately. Hard to confuse Ogham with Latin,” and he looked at both of them accusingly.

“You have to hold it in the light,” and Dell produced his cell phone and lit it up. Hill turned the box until he caught it just right, and then his eyebrows rose. “I’ll be damned.”

“So it’s nice, right?”

“Nice? This is downright art.” Hill pulled the box to his desk and switched on a reading lamp. “Whoever did this is a genius.”

Drew felt a little excitement rising. “What do you mean?”

“You have Ogham and Latin script blending into each other, one or the other visible depending on how you hold it. Gamers would kill for this. You could probably get five hundred for it.”

“The vast Becker fortune,” Dell murmured, and Drew’s excitement deflated. “So what does it say?”

“Well ...” Hill pulled the box to the light and

tilted it back and forth, "... it says ... huh, how 'bout that?"

"What, something about a car warranty?" Dell deadpanned and they all chuckled.

"That's funny," Hill agreed, "but no. This isn't standard Latin. It's Vulgar."

"It's dirty?" Drew was amused at that. "Dad picks up a box of Latin dirty jokes. Of course."

"No. It's local, not standard. You know, like speaking redneck, which is English, but, well," and he waggled his hand.

"Okay." Drew understood. "But it's still Latin, right? You can still read it, right?"

"Well, yes, but give me a minute." Hill scrutinized the box, turning it here and there, blinked, put it down, and laughed.

Great, Drew thought, a dirty joke after all. "So, what's the joke?"

"Oh, it's not a joke. Roughly, it says, 'Whoever holds the great sword Excalibur shall rule the kingdom.'"

"Oh, great." Dell threw his hands up. "King Arthur crap. So it *is* a *Dungeons & Dragons* thing." He gave Drew a wry look. "Dad's talents never cease to amaze."

Drew had to agree, but what in the world was a D&D artifact doing in Dad's WW2 locker? "Is that what the Ogham says?"

"Doubtful," Hill said as he picked the box back up. "Ogham is mainly names, usually on boundary stones." He tilted the box in the light. "Hmm," he said, after a moment, "it's definitely not Viking. Looks Old Irish ..." and he tsked. "This is definitely a joke."

"What?" Drew and Dell asked at the same time. But did not punch each other's shoulders because this wasn't the place. Later, maybe.

"It's Merlin's name."

"Merlin? Oh, fine," Dell said, and tapped Drew on the arm. "Let's just give it to one of our geek nephews and be done with this thing."

"So it actually says 'Merlin,' huh?" Drew said, unable to hide his disappointment. He knew that Merlin was a modern name, not some ancient one, which meant this box was, at best, ten or twenty years old, when D&D was in its heyday. Five hundred dollars, though, nothing to sneeze at.

"No, it's the Latinized version." And he held the box up dramatically and toned, "Merlinus Ambrosius." And instantly dropped the box, grabbing his wrist and yelping, "Ow!"

Drew could see why. The box had landed on its side and was smoking, with what looked like a burning fuse in the middle chasing around the box. "What the hell?"

Dell said nothing, simply dropped to the floor as if the box was a bomb. Which was a pretty good conclusion, and Drew dropped alongside and pulled his arms and knees together so he could kiss his ass goodbye.

There was a *pop* and a fizzing, and the room filled with sulfur smoke. So, the box was packed with matches that were so old the presence of the reading lamp had been enough to set it off. Any second, the smoke alarm would sound, the whole building emptied, and he and Dell charged with wanton vandalism. Fortunately, that didn't happen.

After a few moments of no further devastating

pops, Drew noted the smoke was dissipating and, cautiously, unwound and pulled himself up the desk to peer over it. Hill was still sitting in his chair, holding his hand, a shocked expression on his face as he stared down at the box, smoke still drifting out of a black line that now showed in the middle. Drew stood, not making any sudden movements, aware that Dell also came to his feet, but ensured Drew stayed between him and the box. Love you, too.

"What happened?"

Hill flapped his hand at Drew. "It burned me." Accusation in his voice. Drew made the 'not me!' gesture. "Professor Hill, I had no idea what this thing would do."

Hill scowled as if he expected a trick, but Dell leaned over the desk and poked the box. "So it's not a bomb?"

"Well, if it were, you would have just set it off," Drew pointed out, and then all three of them leaned over it. "Gotta be some kind of prank box."

"I'll sue whoever made it," Hill declared and eyed them suspiciously, but Drew 'not-me'd' that, too. "We're just as mystified as you are, Professor."

"It's open," Dell said.

"Huh?" Drew looked at him, but Dell reached down and pulled at the box. Drew braced for what would probably be a much bigger explosion, or poison gas or something, and after a moment, Dell had the top half of the box off and laid it beside the other. After a few moments of not dying, they all leaned in.

The inside was lined with dark blue velvet, and folded neatly in the middle was a piece of paper.

Wait ... not paper. Something else ...

"Parchment," Hill toned and fumbled around in his desk for something.

"How medieval," Drew said, and he and Dell looked at each other and frowned. This little goof was getting weirder by the moment.

"Ah," Hill produced a pair of oversized tweezers with cushioned ends. "I use this for handling valuable documents."

"You think this is a valuable document?" Dell asked, dollar signs in his eyes.

Hill shrugged and gingerly grasped an end of the parchment and carefully, very carefully, inch by inch, levered it to the top of the box. With his free hand, he fumbled about his desk and spread a cloth, and then placed the parchment on top of it. It fell over like a folded Post-It note, symbols bleeding through in a thick blue ink. Drew reached for it, but Hill said, "Tut! Let me use these." Carefully, he took a corner of the parchment and teased it apart, little by little, with such consummate skill that Drew concluded he must paint figurines. For D&D. Funny how that keeps coming up.

Eventually, Hill had the entire parchment unfolded, and he flipped it over. "Don't breathe on it, if you can," Hill warned. Silly advice. Drew and Dell were too eager and crowded the space, giving each other a Moe and Curly head bump.

Bunch of ink lines.

"Are these words?" Drew asked Hill, who had pulled out a magnifying glass, examining the parchment like some old-style professor in some B-movie. "No," he said, "at least not any words I recognize. But I'll tell you," and he blinked hard, "it looks like a map."

"This?" Dell flicked a finger. "Not like any map I ever saw."

"Well, not a modern map, obviously." An element of dismissiveness in Hill's voice made Dell frown. "But that's what it is. See?" He pointed at the lines. "This is a circular lake. And these are mountains or hills surrounding the lake." He pursed his lips. "I'd say it's England."

"Why would you say it's England? Could be Germany, for all we know." Drew pointed out.

"Except for Merlin's name."

Drew had to give him the point. "Okay. So where in England?"

Hill shrugged. "Beats me. I'd guess Wales or Cornwall, going with the Arthurian legends, but it really could have been anywhere." He frowned. "Was your Dad ever in England?"

"Well, yeah, dubya dubya two and all that." Drew replied, "I guess he got staged in England."

"Do you happen to know where?"

"Eh." Drew flicked that away. "Don't know. He never really talked about it. Said something once about a castle nearby, with a nice walled area around it."

"Walled area, huh?" Hill mused. "Wouldn't by chance be Denbeigh Castle, would it?"

Drew and Dell made mutual shrugs, and Drew asked, "Why?"

"Because it's in Wales. Not too far from traditional sites associated with the Lady of the Lake. Who has the sword, you know."

"Really." Drew was not impressed by that, but noted a mild stirring of internal interest. All of this seemed a far-fetched stretch, but interesting how these disparate and far-flung facts seemed to mesh a bit. At their ends, anyway ....

.... *clank, clank, clank* ...

"What in the world?" Hill looked up, staring at the door. Sounded to Drew like someone was dragging an anvil down the hall. He was about to ask if they had metal-working classes on this floor when the door shattered into glass and wood shrapnel, spraying the room like a grenade as the center of the door collapsed inward, as if someone had kicked it.

Someone had.

A knight. Or a reasonable facsimile of one: chainmail shirt that ran all the way to the knees with a leather vest over it, big sword and helmet with a golden mask depicting a clean-shaven youth covering the face, but all of it old; the chainmail rusted, the helmet and facemask tarnished, the sword chipped, and rents in the vest. The knight had a shield, a round one with a rusty boss in the middle.

Drew thought someone was having them on, maybe some D&D nutcase who wanted the Druid Box for further adventures. Except for the shattered door and the sudden raising of the sword at Dell's head.

"Crap!" Drew yelled and pitched his chair at the idiot gamer with a strength and force he didn't know he could muster. Maybe Dell's pending skull-split gave him the adrenaline, but no matter, it worked. The chair caught the knight on the downward swing of the sword and drove him into the doorframe. Dell, never one to shirk a good barfight, picked up his chair and cracked the knight upside the head, driving the helmet into the wall like a sledgehammer, and the brothers scampered a safer distance into the room as the knight collapsed, its helmet rolling away ...

... and revealing a skull.

Really decent makeup job, Drew thought, but far too decent because this was a skinny skull with an even skinnier neck bone, so what? What? How do you make a mask like that?

And then the skull dissolved, as did the rest of the knight.

They stood tableau, Drew and Dell side by side as was their wont in any fight, Hill standing behind his desk, mouth agape, apparently not one to react swiftly when trouble called, staring at the white ash on his floor where a knight used to be. "There's something you don't see everyday," Dell observed.

No, officer, we have no idea who it was—some nut in a knight's getup and he ran away after crashing the door, and yes, provost, you're going to send someone to clean up this mess and replace the door, right? A combination of Drew and Dell and Hill dissuaded the authorities enough they didn't arrest them, or at least take them in for questioning, although the looks in their eyes ranged from suspicion to incredulity, which was probably the same thing. Once all that was over, they were in Hill's basement, the box and parchment on his card table, the three of them sitting around staring at it.

"What the hell?" Drew repeated for about the hundredth time.

"Indeed," Hill responded for the equal number of times.

"I think," Dell interrupted the sequence, "we can safely say that this is legit."

Drew rounded on him. "Legit what?"

"I'm ... not sure. A map?"

"To where?"

"The location of Excalibur."

Drew blew a raspberry, and Hill pursed his lips, and Dell looked at them both. "Seriously? With Moonknight busting in on us like that?"

"I'm not really sure what that was," Drew said.

"Let's say, for the sake of argument," Hill began, "that this is an actual map to the actual location of Arthur's sword. If it is, it's magical, and it stands to reason that there would be magical guardians."

"'Stands to reason' doesn't really apply here," Drew said, dryly.

Hill waved that off. "Yes, yes, I know, but let's be rational and make our first assumption that magic is just technology that we haven't discovered yet ..." Drew and Dell rolled eyes at each other "... and such a valuable artifact should have protectors commensurate with its tech."

Drew blinked at him. "So you're saying we can expect more knightly visits?" Dell smirked at the pun.

"Yes."

They looked around nervously, expecting to hear clanks coming down the basement stairs, but nothing. "All right," Dell said as the moment passed, "can we then all say the map is legit?"

Drew and Hill considered and then nodded their heads.

"Great. So where is it?"

"England," Drew piped.

Dell gave Hill a look, who said, "That's a rather big place, overall, but we can narrow it down to Cornwall or Wales. To a circular lake there."

"How many circular lakes are in Cornwall and Wales?" Drew asked.

Hill offered 'who knows?' shoulders.

"Great," Drew concluded, "any way to narrow it down even more?"

Hill peered at the map. "This," he carefully pointed at the south of the lines, "looks like a hilltop." He pulled out another magnifying glass—how many did this guy have?—and studied the drawing for a bit. "You see what looks like a smudge over the hilltop? Yes? It's a pointing finger."

"Really?" Drew leaned in, and Hill warded him. "Not so close. This is delicate." Drew tsked and adjusted so he could see through the lens and, yeah, how 'bout that? A tiny little finger pointing at the hilltop. "Okay, X marks the spot, or finger marks the spot. So where is it?"

"The traditional candidates for the Lady's Lake are Llyn Ogwen in Wales, Dozmary Pool, and The Loe in Cornwall, but I don't think they fit."

"Why not?"

"Dozmary is in the middle of a plain, while The Loe is a ribbon lake. If I had to pick one, it'd be Ogwen."

Dell stared at him suspiciously. "How come you know so much about this?"

"Runes tend to be repetitive, telling the same story."

"And you've read a lot of runes. Okay, I get it,

but I thought they were mostly names.

"And places. Like Ogwen. Arthur and Lady of the Lake. Those."

"Okay, okay," Drew waved Hill's growing irritation down. "You're read up. So what about this Ogwen? Can we Google map it?"

They did, the three of them behind the desk and leaning into the monitor, zooming in and out and generally getting in each other's way, but concluding: "It's not really round." Dell said.

"It's sort of round," Hill said, "at least, the eastern part."

"I'd call it more tadpole-shaped than round. Although, there's a pretty tall mountain to the south, this Tryfan." He tapped the screen and raised his eyebrows at the other.

"Yeah," Drew said with great reluctance and zoomed in, then zoomed out, his frown deepening, then said, "Hey. Look at this one."

He moved the map to the upper left, zoomed in, and a spot of blue came into focus. "Marchlyn Mawr. Now that's round."

"Roundish," Dell conceded.

"And it's got a decent mountain to the south, this Craig ... Kerwriggle, I guess that's how you'd say it."

Hill frowned deeper at the screen. "It's Cwrwgl, which only a Welshman can pronounce, but means 'coracle.'"

"Small, round boat," Drew mused. "Looks sort of like one, doesn't it?"

Hill suddenly stood, the frown remaining. "There's something ..." and he went to one of his overstuffed and messy bookshelves and rummaged about while Dell and Drew watched him with amusement. The very picture of the befuddled professor … "Ah!" He pulled out a dusty old volume and leafed through it for a bit then, "Ah!" again. And a blink of surprise. "This is interesting," he said.

"Okay, Professor, Gilligan and I are all attention," Dell said, and Drew elbowed him for the reference, but Hill only looked at them with some confusion. "There's a story," he finally said. "It's a bit odd. A shepherd found a cave in Craig … Kerwriggle … that he said contained Arthur's treasures." That raised everyone's eyebrows. "He looked out on the lake and saw a coracle drawing near, with three beautiful women looking up at him, but the oarsman was terrifying, so he ran away."

"Understandable," Drew commented, "I'd run away, too."

"But at least with an armful of treasure," Dell pointed out.

"Not if I was terrified."

"The confusion," Hill interrupted what was turning into a pointless argument, "comes from the location. This is supposed to have happened on Llyn Ogwen."

"But Kerwriggle is above the Mawr there," Drew said as he tapped the screen.

"Maybe it can be seen from Ogwen," Dell suggested.

"That's Tryfan." And another argument was about to ensue when Hill raised his hand. "Mawr is round," and he indicated the map still open on the desk.

They considered. They compared. And then concluded. “Can we get a flight to Wales tonight?” Drew asked.

They could, sort of, from Love Field, but not until the early morning, with stops either at Kennedy or Atlanta, depending on the flight, then Cardiff, on KLM. For about 2k each.

“Not bad,” Drew said, but Dell snorted. “This thing better be worth it. I’ve maxxed my credit card.” Like Drew had never heard that before.

“So I guess the question is, Kennedy or Atlanta?”

“Atlanta. Kennedy sucks,” Dell voted.

“And Atlanta doesn’t?” Drew shook his head. “Let’s just see what flight Hill picks. Then we’ll pick the other.” Dell laughed.

They threw their bags in to the back of Drew’s Transit. “You’ve got the box, right?”

Dell tapped his lockable metal suitcase. “Right here.”

“How we gonna get that through Customs?”

Dell shrugged. “Gift for our addled auntie who lives near Tryfan, officer.”

“Kerwriggle. And she’ll have to pay a VAT tax, I think, so we need to have a readily identifiable auntie.”

“You know you just said ‘tax tax,’ right?” Dell said.

“What?”

“Value Added Tax. So it’s got ‘tax’ already in it. That’s like adding ‘team’ to the end of ‘SWAT’.”

“Shut up.” Drew threw his bag on top of Dell’s. “We’ll just have to wing it, I suppose … what?”

Dell had stepped from the back of the van and was frowning down the road, still shrouded in mist and early morning dark. “Do you hear that?”

Clank, clank, clank ...

“Oh crap!” Drew shouted as a sword parted the front of the van through to the asphalt underneath, striking sparks and smashed windshield all over. The sword withdrew, then a pair of mailed hands gripped both sides of the severed van and pulled it apart, leaving the two ends of the front at a ninety-degree angle, like an aircraft that opened in the front. Staring at them was a helmeted knight, but no face mask this time. Oh no. Skull. With blazing red eyes. Aimed right at them.

“Oh, crap!” Dell reiterated and grabbed the metal suitcase out from under Drew’s bag and turned about. “Run, you idiot!” Directed at Drew, who did just that. Thanks for grabbing my bag, too, brother.

Drew reached for it when the knight flexed and, with a screech of metal, the two halves fell apart, canted on their unsupported sides, and Drew’s bag fell to the ground, as well as the spare and the tire iron. Drew slapped at the bag again, but the knight kicked the halves apart, driving them about ten feet away and, man, was this thing strong or what?

Sword raised, it came for Drew, and he grabbed his bag and tossed it at the knight, who fenced it away as if it were nothing and raised the sword again, and Drew’s hand closed on the tire iron. He swung it like a homerun bat, connecting with the knight’s chainmailed ribs, the impact feeling like bone and iron and sending a shock all the way down Drew’s legs.

But not as much of a shock as the knight

suffered, who folded around the tire iron like a marshmallow around a knife, dropping the sword and staggering backward. Drew didn't hesitate, crashing the iron into the thing's skull until it fell over, sighed, and dissolved.

"Okay," Dell said from behind him, "chairs and tire irons kill these things. Do we need to get some garlic and crosses, too?"

"Don't think that'll work. And thanks for the assist, by the way." Drew bent over, gasping, his hands on his knees.

"Don't mention it. The box is still intact." And he flourished the metal suitcase

"That's a load off my mind." Drew stood, getting his breath back, arms on his hips. "How the hell am I gonna explain this to the insurance company?"

"Got a better question." Dell kicked at a piece of bumper. "How the hell we gonna get to the airport?"

Taxi.

The driver pulled up, looked at the parted van, shrugged, and got them to the terminal in decent time. They found Hill fuming at the counter. "What took so long?"

"We made a knight of it," Drew said.

Dell chortled and then told Hill what happened, who went pale. "Nothing attacked me."

"You don't have the map." Dell nudged his suitcase.

Hill frowned. "You don't intend to check that in, do you?"

"It's locked."

Hill cocked an eyebrow in disbelief, and Drew

had to admit he made a silent point. Hill opened his soft-sided briefcase. "Put it in here. We'll take it as a carry-on."

Both Drew and Dell regarded him silently. "No offense, Professor," Drew said mildly, "but we don't really know you."

Hill blinked, then his mouth fell open. "You think I would steal it?" He looked genuinely hurt, and the brothers immediately felt bad. "It's not like I can outrun you or anything."

"This is true," Dell acknowledged.

Which seemed to hurt the Professor even more, and he tsked. "I also don't think I would do as well against the knights as you two."

That decided it. The brothers looked sheepish and apologized, but Hill was still hurt, even when the brothers chose to go through Atlanta with him, which should have been some sign of trust, hey?

As they went through TSA, the officer had Hill remove the box and looked at it. "What's this?"

"Gift for our auntie," Drew said, and the officer pursed his lips and waved them through. Hill still wore a hurt expression when they made it to the gate, so they decided to appease him with his expertise. "So what do you think those knights are?" Drew asked.

Hill warmed to it. "Guardians, like I said. I think they're the Knights of the Round Table."

"What?" Drew was somewhat incredulous. "You mean like Lancelot?"

"Not at that level. I think these are the lower knights, like Agravain and Geraint."

"Who?"

"Precisely."

"So we haven't even met the A team yet. Great."

Atlanta was a stupid choice because it was a local requirement that any connecting flight must be on the other side of the airport, which meant shuttles and trains and escalators and fighting with about ten thousand other people in just as much of a hurry as them, and, with seconds to spare, they grabbed their row, Drew at the window, Dell in the aisle seat, with Hill in the middle.

Hill kept the briefcase on his lap, putting it under the seat when an attendant frowned at him, but putting it back when the plane lifted.

To give KLM its due, the flight was decent. The food, the Dutch stewardesses ... Dell and Drew continuously fist-bumped over Hill across the Atlantic until Hill rolled his eyes and said, "Would you knock it off?"

"Sorry, Professor, we have a genetic imperative." Drew nodded in shared appreciation at Dell. "And all this appreciation has made me restless, so I'm going to freshen up."

Which meant Hill and Dell had to move out of his way, and Drew ended up with the briefcase as Hill and Dell reseated, and he held on to it, "I'll take this with me," to Hill's consternation, but Dell said, "Where's he going to go?"

The back latrine, of course, and had to give KLM its due, spacious. Could actually turn around in there without breaking an elbow. Drew did his business and admired himself in the mirror—not bad for forty, still have the hair, acceptable paunch, and the crow's feet give me the air of experience—and then opened the briefcase and removed the box and studied it. What in the world had he gotten himself into? You'd think an air-of-experienced forty-year-old would have thought twice before launching into a half-baked adventure. But he didn't think twice in other situations, and now had been divorced twice. "Make you proud, Dad," he said to the mirror, and then looked at the box. "Might make you prouder." He chuckled and put the box in the briefcase, and opened the door to a knight standing there watching him with red skull eyes.

"Crap," Drew said.

In the time he took to say that, the knight drove his sword straight at Drew's midsection. Drew dodged, but not quite fast enough. The sword poked through his jacket, barely missing his ribcage and causing him to slam his right arm against the mirror, shattering it. "*Ack*!" That hurt!

Spinning on his toes, Drew threw the bifold door closed as the knight plunged again, catching the blade as it drove through the fold. Drew saw his chance. Yanking the door open with the blade caught in the middle, he rolled an elbow at the knight's head, which also hurt—helmet, you idiot—and did nothing but annoy Sir Skullface, who tugged at the sword to free it. Drew grasped the hilt and helped the knight yank it back hard, driving the pommel straight into Skullface's skull. That had a decided effect as Skull fell back against the food warmer. Drew did not hesitate, turned the blade around and drove it into the thing's chest.

It fell. It turned to dust. Just in time for the converging attendants to circle him, stare at his bleeding arm, and then at the wrecked door.

"I had some trouble getting out," Drew said.

Cardiff Customs and Security and the airport medics were not amused. The three of them spent a lot more time in detention than a simple door wreckage called for, but several persons wanted to know how the door had malfunctioned and how Drew had managed to tear it off its top hinges. Attributing that to Sir Skullface wasn't a good idea, so Drew had to explain, over and over, to various engineers and KLM reps and police, the made-up movements he thought best explained it, which all of the engineers and reps said was impossible; but look, there's a broken door and broken mirror what other explanation was there, an attack by a ghost knight?

Then Drew whimpered and held his wounded arm, and the reps looked at each other, whispered the Dutch equivalent of "lawsuit" to each other, and that ended it. One advantage, there was little attention paid to their carry-ons and luggage, just a wave through, and they were standing outside with the onset of early evening. And jet lag.

"Think we're safe?" Drew said, scrutinizing the curb for ghost knights.

"It attacked you on a plane," Dell pointed out, and Drew had to concede that it was easier to skewer them on the sidewalk than in an aircraft bathroom.

"So maybe we should get off the street," Drew

said, "I'm for a hotel room and about fifteen hours of sleep."

"Where they can finish us off in private," Dell pointed out.

Drew was getting really tired of his cogent points. "Look, I need to sleep. We've been up for what, about 20 hours now?" Drew was almost ready to accept a sword through the gut if it meant rest.

"That's a good idea," Hill said, "if we go to sleep now, then we'll be synced with the local time." He gestured at the dropping night. "And then we can figure out how to get to Kerwriggle." He looked around. "There's a Holiday Inn over there."

There was. "Complete with hot and cold running ghost knights," Dell said.

"Look, man," Drew was impatient, "The knights are going to come regardless. So I vote sleep, food, and figure out what we're going to do, in that order. And we all stay in one room for safety."

"Sure. Easier to round us up," Dell said and waved Drew's resultant tsk away. "Okay, agree, we need to get organized, and you're a little whiny bitch when you're tired, so let's go over there."

Drew put down his case. "I'll show you a whiny bitch." He raised fists.

"Combative, too," Dell observed.

"This is not helping," Hill interposed, his exasperation evident.

After a moment, Drew lowered his hands and had to admit that Dell was accurate in his personality assessments. "Fine." He looked at Hill. "Say, Professor, since we're all going to be in the same room, you're not going to make a move on us or anything, are you?"

Hill blinked at them like an owl. "What?"

"Just so things are clear. Not that there's anything wrong with that." He and Dell kept their faces blank.

Hill regarded them for a moment, then slowly shook his head. "Children. I'm with children." He picked up the case and, in a huff, threw it on top of his cart and pushed toward the hotel. The brothers smirked at each other and followed when Hill suddenly stopped, grabbing frantically at the case. "Oh no!" he whispered in a panicked voice.

"What?" From Drew, with rising panic, as Hill scrambled at the case and yanked it open, a look of sheer terror on his face, now matching the one on Hill's ... until he reached quietly into the case and presented the box to them, a small smile on his face.

"That wasn't funny," Dell said.

"Actually, it was pretty good." Drew held up his hands in surrender. "Okay, we'll stop messing with you."

Hill nodded, mission accomplished, and they pushed on.

"You want to go where?"

"And do what?"

The tour guides/outfitters/proprietors of the outdoor shop were twins, fiercely Welsh with red poofy hair that indicated an Ethiopian ancestor, buried somewhere back in the Celtic/Viking/Irish forbears, had produced such a deep red and hairy people. Beards and mustaches and eyebrows so thick one could rappel from them, but with incongruously black eyes that looked at the three of them with some disbelief.

“Here.” Drew tapped the map he had just bought. “And climb this ... Kerwriggle.”

The twins blinked and looked at each other. “It's pronounced ...” and the right twin made a sound like a throat singer warming up, “... and it’s a bit far from here.”

“Snowdonia.” The left twin added.

“Dinorwig.” The right one provided clarification, and the twins exchanged satisfied glances.

“Okay.” Drew had no idea what they meant and looked to Hill for assistance. Not Dell; he was turned about and watching the front of the store, ghost knight lookout. None had bothered them through the night spent with the brothers in the queen bed and Hill on the fold-out couch. Not that Drew would have noticed. He had slept so deeply that a ghost knight could have pinned him to the mattress without him stirring.

“All the more reason to be careful,” Dell said through breakfast and showers, and locating this shop, then the taxi ride to it. Drew almost wished the knights would appear so Dell would shut up about it.

“Yes,” Hill said, “that place. Dinorwig. How far is it?”

“About 180 miles,” said Right.

“You guys use miles?” Drew asked.

“Yes.” Right looked at him askance. “This is the UK, brother.”

“Oh. Yeah. So is there a train?”

Both Left and Right grimaced and raised shoulders. “Yes, brother,” said Right, “but it’s a good six hours. And I don't know when the next one is. Faster by car. Straight up the A470."

"Our cousin," Left said as he whipped out a business card and handed it to Hill, "rents cars. He's just over there." Eyebrow point to the road.

"How fortuitous," Drew said flatly.

Left gave them the quizzical eye. "So what are your plans up there?"

"Uh, you know. Sightsee. Hike. Look around."

"Hmm." More quizzical eye. "The Electric Mountain?"

"The what?" Drew asked, but Hill cut him off with a gesture. "Yes. The Elcctric Mountain. That's where we're going."

"Hmm." Simultaneously from the twins, who had crossed two hairy arms below their beards and gimlet eyes. "Look at that, Arwen," Left said to Right, "Americans came all the way here to see the Electric Mountain."

"That's something it is, Carwyn," Right to Left. "And them with that Hoover Dam over there."

Arwyn nodded vigorously. "And that Grand Canyon."

"Niagara." Carwyn pursed his lips. "Easier trip to there than here."

"That's so," Arwyn agreed, "people from all over the world go there to see those. Not a lot come here to see Electric Mountain." And the gimlet eyes locked on Drew.

"Okay. So, we like mountains. Electric or otherwise." Drew said, lamely.

"Hmm." The twins studied them.

"You know, Arwyn," Carwyn said, "some tough country up there."

"That it is."

"And look at them." Flourish of the hairy hands taking in the three, even the watchful Dell, "Don't look very much like hikers and outdoorsmen."

"Now wait a minute—" Drew was rather offended because he kept in shape, but Hill put a hand on his arm. "Maybe we could use some help in that department?" he asked.

The twins beamed at them. "Well, then, you've come to the right place. We'll make sure you have everything you need." Arwyn flipped a hand at the shop.

"For certain!" Carwyn chortled. "You'll so look the part that no one, no one at all, would question you." A pause, as the twins regarded them for a moment. "Right this way, gentlemen," Arwyn came out from the counter and waved them to the back.

"Oh," said Arwyn, pulling out another business card, "when you get to Dinorwig, look up our cousin, Dylan. He's a guide."

"A good one." Carwyn underscored.

"He'll be expecting you," Arwyn turned to the terminal on the counter and began typing furiously.

"Indeed he will."

As Drew followed Carwyn to the piles of clothes and equipment, no doubt all of it name-brand and top dollar, he couldn't help feeling like he'd just been rolled.

"This thing better be worth a fortune because we've just spent one," Drew groused as Dell leaned intently into the seat, trying to figure out how to drive on the left without killing them all. Added to the expenses so far was this Mercedes that Cousin Maldwyn insisted they needed for the perilous A470 and, of course, to contain all of their gear. Which it barely did.

"This isn't about getting rich." Hill, buried under coats and backpacks and even a tent, admonished. "It's about history."

"Lucrative history, then. So I don't lose my house." They had used Drew's Visa because Dell remained on knight watch, and Hill had looked at him like he was crazy.

"You don't have to worry about that," Dell said, "because we'll be dead before we reach Kerwriggle."

Sure seemed like it. Tailgating was apparently a legal requirement in Wales, as were excessive speeds and swerving in and out of lanes. Drew was amazed at the traffic in Cardiff. Gridlock and actual jams. What were all these people doing out here, trying to find a fabulous lost treasure? Dell's tendency to revert to right-side driving at the most inopportune moments didn't help. How many times they'd suddenly found themselves head-on with some truck, Drew had lost count. Roundabouts, who came up with those? And cones. My God, the cones. Did Wales pave their roads with cones?

So when they finally got away from city and suburbs, and found themselves in the country, he should have felt better. Except the road was now two lanes with farm tractors around every curve. Or cyclists. Drew wondered how much time in Welsh prison for running one over.

The names on the signs ... "Care Philly," Drew announced at one.

"No, thank you," Dell responded, "I don't care for

Philly."

"Would you care for a Philly cheesesteak?"

"Why yes, yes I would."

"It means 'the fort of Fili,'" Hill offered to absolutely no one's question, proving again the guy had no sense of fun.

A little bit later: "Pointy Prick!"

Which broke Dell up and almost put them under the wheels of a truck. "Philistines," Hill sighed, "it's pronounced ..." and it sounded like he said *Bonty Preeg* or something like that.

"I thought you didn't speak Welsh." Dell was suspicious.

"I don't. I just know the pronunciations."

"Isn't that the same thing?"

"Of course not. If you see J-A-V-I-E-R in Spain, but don't speak Spanish, you still know it's 'Hav-E-air.' "

"It is?" Dell had turned about in mock surprise. "I thought it was Jay-V-are!"

"Please to keep your eyes on the road," Drew braced against his seat as they drifted over.

"Sure, sure," and they were back on the right, or left, or wherever they were supposed to be.

It became, like most drives, a matter of road hypnosis, except this was interesting. Very green, very hilly, with lots of water here and there, and the oddly named towns, most of which looked as if they were built about King Arthur's time. Lots of castles, too.

"The Welsh were a contentious lot, weren't they?" Drew said, a couple of hours into it.

"What makes you say that?" Hill asked.

Drew pointed at the ruins of a castle on a far

ridge.

Hill nodded. “Had to protect themselves from the English.”

“Didn’t we all?” Drew summed and fell into the drive again.

They were getting into mountains as the day began to fade. Not grand, like the Rockies, but decent enough. Drew entertained himself spotting rockfalls and cairns and passes, until Dell said, “Uh oh.”

“What?” And Drew swung about, convinced a ghost knight descended.

“I lost the signal.” Drew tapped the phone set on the dash.

“You expecting a call?”

“No, but I was expecting the map, and now it’s gone.”

Drew shrugged. “We’ll just read the road signs.”

“And how’s that been working out for you, Mr. Pointy Prick?”

“Touché,” and Drew hunched down, scrutinizing the road and the incomprehensible signs. Not helping.

“I think we’re supposed to bear to the right at some point,” Hill offered.

“Any idea what that point may be?” Dell asked.

“I’m guessing where the highway we’re on bears to the left.”

Drew restrained an urge to reach back and slap Hill because they’d already been through quite a few of those leftward bearings so far, but he decided to stay on recon and stared ahead. “I think this may be it up ahead.”

“May be what?”

"The turn." Drew gestured while quickly reading a road sign that whipped by. "Gellily ... something or other." He pointed. "Up ahead."

"Do we have a map?" Dell pawed at the glove box.

"Would you worry about driving instead?" Drew yelped, and Dell scowled at him, and then they were in the middle of an intersection that went left or right and had a tractor in it going right, like they were, and a truck going left, and Dell forgot what country they were in. Somehow, they skidded across the intersection, turned about the wrong way, while the farmer on the tractor shook his fist and yelled something incomprehensible, and the truck blew its horn well past the required display of irritation.

"This is why the knights haven't attacked us," Drew observed, "They know we won't survive."

Spoke too soon.

As Dell maneuvered the car into a more or less legal position, Drew saw three persons standing athwart the road where they probably should have borne right, and he sighed because this was probably Welsh police about to have a word with the Americans and their obvious inability to drive. It was getting dark; it could be three irate farmers, as far as Drew knew. "Turn on the headlights, will you?" Dell did.

Not farmers. Not police.

Three knights.

"Crap," all three of them said simultaneously.

It became a test of Dell's driving prowess, reversing on the wrong side of the road, where he could not see what was coming around the bends, much less what was behind him, but he still jammed it into reverse and floored it. Mostly because the advancing knights were almost on them. Good move for a moment or two because they outran the knights, until Dell went over the intersection and into the ditch, landing in the front yard of some building, the car hitting with the shock of an anvil slamming into each of their backs.

"*Ow*!" said simultaneously.

Which didn't quite express the situation. They were angled about 25° toward the upper slope, the cracked front windshield showing more of the sky than the berm leading up to it, the back of the car jammed solidly into the bracken or heather, or whatever the Brits called this underbrush, the back windshield completely gone, having deposited its fragments all over Hill, who was gingerly brushing it off to avoid cuts. "Everyone alright?" Drew called.

"Hardly," Dell said, trying to extricate his arm and face from the steering wheel, or whatever the Brits called it. "I think we—"

He did not finish the suggestion. There, up on the berm and staring down at them, the three ghost knights. If a bone face could hold an expression, they were gleeful. And mad.

"Do you think they can climb down here?" Hill, worried, stopped brushing glass, leaning forward with the other two to get a better look.

In answer, the three knights, one somewhat forward of the others, stepped off simultaneously down the slope, their greave-encased legs sure and steady on the descent, their swords raised.

"Crap," Drew said, and fell out of the side door. Dell did the same on the driver's side and Hill, well, his door was jammed.

Too bad, Drew thought, gonna miss that guy. Not fun, but had his uses ... except he has the box.

"Crap," Drew said and swung about through the bracken heather and launched at the passenger door while Hill banged on it from the other side. Drew figured they'd have the door open in about five minutes, if the knights would give them the time.

No such luck.

A shudder went through the underbrush above them, and then it parted, and the lead knight stood there, his pals arrayed beside him, all three staring at Drew. The lead knight had more elaborate armour than the other two, at least what Drew could make out from the rusted, rotting, parts of it, filigreed and decked out with extra points that could only be decorative, which meant this knight was more important than the others. So, they'd finally attracted the A- Team.

Skewered by Galahad himself.

"Listen, fellows." Drew raised his hands in supplication as Hill continued his assault on the stuck door. "We're just some schlubs from America. Nothing serious or dangerous. So what do you want from us?"

Galahad's eyes glowed blue, which was a different look, and he turned his helmet-encased head creakily, every vertebra grating as loudly as his armour, and stared at Hill, still trying to force the door. The other two knights followed the gaze, and it was pretty obvious what they wanted.

"Okay then." Keeping his hands up, Drew took giant steps backward, through the bracken stuff, adrenaline giving him the ability to break through it as Hill stopped his efforts, jaw dropped. "Now wait a minute," Hill said.

Galahad stepped to the door as one of the others moved to the other door, and the third covered the front. Not that Hill had any chance of climbing over the seats and getting out that way, but these guys were thorough. Galahad grabbed the door handle, and with the sound of a sardine can opening, pulled the door completely off its hinges and tossed it over his head as if it were said can.

"Crap," Drew said, no longer able to force his way back.

Galahad stared down at the shrinking Hill, who still had the case clutched to his chest. Drew was about to suggest he let the knight have it and maybe they all wouldn't be eviscerated, when *krang!* a rock, a good-sized one, slammed into Galahad's brow, driving him back, more in surprise than injury. Another rock crashed into the back of the other side knight's helmet, forcing him to almost fall over the roof of the car. The front knight was turning to see where the artillery was coming from, when the third rock smacked it upside the head.

Drew knew without Dell's, "How do you like that, you tin foil bastards?" confirming yell: Dell was a class A baseball pitcher, and had apparently found a good supply of missiles. Drew located him standing in the only clearing among all this wilderness, winding up for another throw, which whipped a baseball-sized-and-shaped rock right into Galahad's face, actually knocking him to the ground. "C'mon!" Dell yelled.

Feets, don't fail me now.

Lunging at Hill, Drew grabbed his lapels and yanked him out of the vehicle, the way now more than clear given Galahad's efforts, the two of them collapsing on the ground, bouncing up, and running around the back of the car, Hill still clutching the case. Good for him. Avarice over survival. Drew led the way, breaking through and clearing the car, just as the passenger door knight stood up from the shellacking Dell had just delivered, saw what they were doing, and swung his sword viciously at Drew's head just at the moment another good-sized stone caught it in the side of the helmet. The blade whistled past, just cutting Drew's ear.

Cold. So cold.

The shock of that almost dropped Drew to his knees. The frost ran down his ear and seized his heart: never had Drew ever experienced such a wash of loneliness and despair and desperation. "God!" he shouted, his vision now lost in black hills and empty skies in which there was no rest, no peace. The only reason he kept going was Hill's determined hand in his lower back. "Go! Go!" the professor urged, and Drew recovered and redoubled because, oh Lord.

In seconds, with a speed impelled by fear, they bracketed Dell, who had scooped up another perfectly formed rock and stood ready. "You all right?" he asked, staring at what must be Drew's bloody ear.

"Don't let them touch you with their swords. Just don't," Drew gasped, returning mostly to this dimension. Mostly.

Which looked exactly what the three knights

wanted to do, sword touch them, that is. They had moved to the side of the car and faced them, eyes glowing red now, even Galahad's, swords up before their faces like upheld crosses. Through some unheard signal, the three stepped forward simultaneously, pushing through the underbrush as if it was nothing.

"You two might want to assist," Dell suggested as he whirled his stone at Galahad, who merely flicked his head aside to miss it.

Good idea. Drew and Hill armed themselves with other rocks, of which, fortunately, there seemed to be a lot, and hurled them, Drew almost as good as Dell. Hill about as good as Obama. It was quite a volley once the three of them got started, and Drew watched with some satisfaction, the ghost knights temporarily stymied, until they swatted the stones out of the air, the clash of metal turning their missiles into bright flashes of dust.

"Like I said, don't let the swords hit you," Drew emphasized as he picked up another stone to toss.

"Perhaps we should run," Hill offered, and yes, perhaps they should, but where? Drew took a quick look behind and noted this clearing was the end of a driveway that stretched to the farmhouse and outbuildings he'd glimpsed as they reversed themselves over the berm. From where a very large man dressed in overalls, checked shirt, and big flappy hat, was storming in their direction, yelling something that sounded like "twim fats!" and other words incomprehensible to Drew, while shaking a very large walking stick, the intent being very clear.

Just don't need this right now.

The knights paused as the man cleared the ridge

and came into their view, which stopped the man dead in his tracks, his eyes popped, mouth open, and good, this might give us a couple of more minutes to live, when the knights faded away as Drew watched. Just gone, like the evening sunlight.

Well, okay.

The farmer ran up, stick at the ready. "Were those knights?" he asked in somewhat understandable English, his astonishment rendering him more articulate.

Dell shrugged. "Think there's a Renaissance fair in town."

Turned out the farmer had been yelling the Welsh word *twmffats*, the local way of calling someone a superior idiot. Given the situation, it was probably justified. Stupid Americans who don't know how to drive to begin with, driving on the wrong side, can't even negotiate a simple turn, and scared the heck out of fairgoers. Also turned out the farmer was a cousin some part removed from Carwyn and Darwyn and Dylan of Dinorwig and, after a few phone calls, and belated arrivals of tow trucks and other vehicles, Drew's main card was maxxed, as was half of his other card. But the three of them were ensconced, by four in the morning, in a little tourist house in a town called Llanberis, very close to the Electric Mountain.

"See you gentlemen in the morning. Later morning, anyways," and Dylan walked into the dark, chuckling over the various receipts and reimbursements he and his cousins had received over the last twelve hours.

"We gonna wait for him?" Drew, his wallet smarting, made an irritated gesture at the closed door, which had no effect on the wind blowing directly underneath it.

"He knows the way," Hill said, pulling out a brand-new parka that Drew had paid for, throwing it on.

"He definitely knows the way to the Electric Mountain, which, by the way, is just across the parking lot, but that's not where we're going, so what do we need a guide for?" Drew tapped the trail map that Dylan had solicitously left them, for a fee. "Dinorwig is up here. And Kerwriggle is over here next to it." He pointed to a spot to the right of the town, in the middle of what was probably quite forbidding territory.

The other two leaned over the map. "Seems a bit of a distance," Hill mused.

"All the more reason we leave now."

"Let's just hold up a minute," Dell whined, or whinged, given where they were. "I've got whiplash from the car wreck and from throwing stones at ghost knights. Plus I haven't eaten in a day. You're missing half an ear, and that looks like major surgery and antibiotics to fix. Let's get our sea legs back before we go hiking all the hell over godforsaken Wales." And he flopped back on the bed. Which was more like a hayrick than a bed. Hill shrugged and dropped down on the floor, comforted by the thick parka.

"And what exactly do we tell Cousin Dylan when he gets here in a few hours? Sorry, mate, changed our minds, we'd like to hike up Kerwriggle and find King Arthur's treasure. Do you mind? And the

Cousin Telegraph would be in full contact mode within seconds, and we'd have the whole damn clan with us."

Dell sighed audibly. "Might be worth it. The knights don't seem to like it when civilians are around."

"At the point they joined us on the expedition, they'd no longer be civilians. Just extra shares."

Silence for a moment, and then Dell cursed and yelled and got up and kicked Hill, who was no happier than him, off the floor. "Call an Uber," Dell ordered. Drew did, surprised someone was still offering service at this time, but maybe this was a partying town. Just one more entry on the card at this point.

When the car pulled up, Drew walked up to the window. "You're not related to Dylan and Carwyn and Arwyn, are you?"

The driver spat out the window. "Those bastards?"

They got in.

By sunrise, the three of them stood before a sheepfold. Sheepfold. Where in the world have we landed, Captain Kirk? Fortunately, there were no sheep in it or anywhere around. Good. Drew wasn't sure how he'd deal with them.

"I think we go this way." Dell had the map, comparing it to the local terrain, looking about, and no kidding, Daniel Boone, there was only one trail leading to the peaks and ridges, and terrible country ahead of them. We are gonna die, Drew thought. "Where's Kerwriggle?"

Dell studied the map for a moment and then twisted and turned in the reddening dawn and finally pointed at a crappy mass of forbidding rocks and ridges off to the south. "I think that's it."

"You think?" Drew was only half incredulous because, by this time, he was resigned to this being the most half-assed seat-of-the-pants blundering around like a blind man expedition ever held in history. Shackleton looked like Pizarro by comparison.

Dell shrugged, no more convinced than Drew, surveyed the area, and said, "We gotta go east, follow this trail. Then, when we see the reservoir, we have to cut to the south. Looks like it gets pretty rough there, the trail ends. We'll have to go cross-country." He frowned at the map. "What's this Pillar of Elidar?"

"I don't know. Let me consult my memory from the last time I was here."

"Smartass," Dell said, and took out his cell but, of course, no signal. He shook the map and looked at Hill. "You have any contributions?"

Hill took the map and studied the portion Dell indicated. "It's probably a prominent feature that we will recognize once we see it, based on its name, and which will let us know where Kerwriggle is."

"Told you this guy was smart," Dell said.

Drew was about to point out that he had never said anything like that from the beginning of this ill-fated trip, but Dell reached among the packs piled up at their feet and pulled out several of the various energy bars they had bought from the only all-night food mart in Wales—apparently—making sure to buy coffee for their Uber guy, Winston, who needed an extra tip to bring them to this location, and an even bigger tip to ensure he kept his mouth shut about it.

There goes the second credit card. "Eat up, boys, we're going to need the fuel for this death march." He tore enthusiastically into the bar, and Drew followed, driven more by starvation than taste because, gawd, this stuff was awful.

Hill's sour face showed a similar conclusion. "Maybe we don't need to take all of this with us," he said, pointing a half-eaten bar at the bags and sling and packs scattered all about them.

"We paid for it," Dell said, unwrapping another bar.

What do you mean 'we,' paleface? Drew thought.

"We may have to take it as a loss, then, because this will slow us down."

Dammit. Hill made sense. Drew mourned the mass of money he had spent so that sheep could enjoy a comfortable night in a nylon tent and sub-zero sleeping bags, and then rummaged around them to salvage what was necessary: water, walking stick, the parka, and boots, because this promised to be rough and cold. The others did the same and, with a backward glance at the booty left behind which, no doubt, some grateful hiker will stumble across, Drew led them away.

'Death march' was an understatement.

The trail dropped at first, which was nice, but then mounted at an angle akin to an Everest ascent. And it was a trail designed by sadists: rocks and furrows and loose areas, and the sun rose and looked at them and laughed and decided to beat them mercilessly. They sweated through their jackets and then froze under the knife-like wind.

Drew's ear hurt. "How far have we gone?" he puffed.

"Maybe a mile," Dell puffed back.

Oh, lovely.

"What do we do if the knights show up?"

Hill and Dell exchanged glances, then both looked at Drew's ear.

"Die, I suppose," Dell said. "What did you say about that sword hit?"

"It's like a Morgul blade," Drew replied. No further explanation necessary. They all got the reference.

They ascended ridges with mind-and-leg numbing efficiency until, somewhere around noon, with the sun laughing hysterically by that time, they cleared a ridgetop and, "Wow," Drew said.

They overlooked Marchlyn Mawr, which was a blue cabochon set deep in stone fittings, with a thick band of concrete lining one end. "That's a serious reservoir," Dell observed.

"Indeed," Hill underscored that and clawed at another water bottle, which he was going through like they were scattered around the terrain just waiting to be harvested.

"Take it easy," Drew warned. "We have no idea where the next water stop is."

"Especially because we're leaving this trail and heading cross-country." Dell pointed south.

Oh, lordy. "Kerwriggle's that way?"

"The Pillar is. At least that's the closest point to us without going all the way around." He traced a finger line around the reservoir where another trail was visible above the concrete and winding its way east …

Reservoir.

Drew smacked his forehead with enough force to give himself a concussion. “We’re idiots. We’re all idiots.” He stamped and cursed and yelled to the heavens, and the other two stared at him like he had lost his mind. Which he had.

“What ails you?” Dell asked, rather mildly. He was used to these outbursts. Not Hill, who quailed behind him, unsure if violence was in the offing.

It was.

“It’s a reservoir!” Drew sputtered, jabbing his hand at the lake below.

“Yes?” Dell, still mild.

“Don’t you get it?” Drew threw quasi-violent hands at them, causing Hill to further quail. “It’s only round because they built a dam across it!” A final dramatic and truly violent point at the water.

It took them about a moment. “Oh,” Hill said, “oh my.”

“Yes, oh my!” Drew sat down heavily on a convenient boulder, thoroughly disgusted.

Dell was quiet for moment. “Look, that doesn’t mean it hasn’t always been round.”

“Does it?” A backhand at the water. “You willing to bet a further search of this godawful rockheap in the offhand chance that this manmade lake was as round a thousand years ago as it is today?” He shook his head miserably. “We have no idea what we’re doing.”

Dell stood on the edge of the slope, staring down at the water. Probably trying to conjure a round lake that coincided with the scroll map. “What’s that?” he asked.

"What's what?" Drew sat head in hands, refusing to play any more reindeer games.

"That." Dell was insistent. "Coming toward us."

Oh, great. Must be more knights on their way, laughing themselves silly over idiots thinking a lake that was round today was round when the map was drawn. He slid around and glared at the lake. And stopped. "What's that?"

In the middle of the reservoir, a dark object bobbed. No, wait, rowed, heading toward the shore below them. They all squinted at it. "Can't really tell," Hill said, "but it looks like a coracle."

They knew that referencc, too, and all tried to make out details. "Didn't we buy binoculars?" Dell asked.

What do you mean, 'we?' Dell thought again and, yes, they had, at Arwyn's insistence, big freakin' expensive 50s, and they were probably sitting in the pile of equipment made as gift to the sheep, but, no, Hill pulled them out of his jacket.

"You brought those?" Drew was somewhat derisive because, dude, no wonder you're so thirsty, but also glad that not all his financial sacrifice was in vain.

"Thought we might need them," Hill said and brought them up and settled and focused. And turned white as a sheet.

"What?" Drew asked, but did not wait for an explanation. Instead, he snatched the glasses off Hill's neck, almost strangling him in the process, and brought the binocs up and focused.

Three women in white robes stood in the prow. Stunning, beautiful women, girded with golden belts and ropes and wearing amber and green jewelry, looking right at him, smiling beatifically. And the guy in the back sculling ...

Drew blanched, then handed the glasses to Dell, who also looked and blanched. "We need to go," Drew concluded, "we need to go right now."

Hastily, because it was very important to be on the other side of the ridges before that thing poling the boat reached the shore and escorted the sisters up for a party. Perhaps they could lose them up here.

Sure.

Fear as a motivator is effective for the short bursts of energy they needed to clear the trail and zip through the boulder fields and rock lines until they were out of sight of the reservoir, but once they had done so, they were spent. More than spent. Drew was ready to fall right down right there and sleep for a few days. The sculler can have him. Probably for lunch.

"Now what?" Drew gasped at the others, who were in no better shape than he, sitting on boulders and gasping even louder.

"Think we can now safely say this is the right round lake," Dell managed, somewhat dryly. Yeah, yeah, let's get past that, shall we.

Hill pulled himself to an overhanging shelf and peered at the distant formations. "I think that's it."

"Kerwriggle?"

"No, the Pillar." And he pointed.

What else could you call that formation but a pillar? It wasn't exactly standing alone and proud in the middle of a field, but was distinct from the godawful murder mountain behind it. "And the mountain behind it is Kerwriggle," Hill concluded.

Of course it was.

"You sure?" Drew asked, really more to buy time than confirm anything.

"Positive." The three of them studied the Pillar and, yeah, that's what it was, so murder mountain. Hill cleared his throat. "You know, it's funny, but there's a legend about Elidir."

"Of course there is," Drew snarked, "and of course you know it."

"Well, I do," Hill snarked back, "and it might be something. Elidir was a monk cruclly mistreated by his fellows, so he ran away, and the fairy folk took him in. Supposedly, if you can find him, you can find the entrance to the fairylands."

"How do you know all these things?" Dell was genuinely curious.

Hill paused. "I don't have a social life."

Big surprise there. "So that's the way into the fairylands, where King Arthur and his pals are making merry, and all we have to do is find a way in." He shook his head. "And just how are we supposed to do that? Without running into the knights and whatever's coming for us across the water there." He shuddered.

"I don't know," Hill said.

"I thought you knew everything."

"Not this." And he gave Drew a dismissive look, then fished the scroll out of the case. "Let's see if this helps." He unrolled it, and the other two joined him to stare and peer and scrutinize the map, and compare it to the terrain but nothing was apparent. "I don't know," Hill said with some exasperation, "maybe we don't have the right perspective," and he held the map up against the murder mountain.

A blue light glowed behind the Pillar.

"What the hell?" Dell and Drew said at the same time, and Hill said, "What?" and dropped the map, and the light disappeared.

"You didn't see that?" Drew asked.

"See what?"

Dell pointed at the mountain. "That light up there."

"What light?"

"Well, it's gone now."

All three of them looked at the scroll. Slowly, Hill raised it, peering over the top of it as the other two fixed on the mountain. As the scroll reached eye level, the blue light stuttered and then came into view.

"That's truly creepy," Drew observed.

"Have you marked the location?" Hill asked.

"Yep. Got it."

"Good." Hill rolled the scroll back into the case. "Let's go, then."

"Sure," Drew said because, really, what else were they going to do now, "but what is that up there?"

Dell shrugged. "The entrance to fairyland." And he followed Hill down the slope toward the bottom of the Pillar.

By the time they reached the base of it, the sun was setting, and this was absolutely the last place on Earth Drew wanted to spend a night, with ghost knights and coracle horrors roaming the area. But it looked as though they were, because ... "No way we're climbing that," Drew concluded, looking up the murder mountain in the fading light.

The other two assented with their silence. It was just too steep and rocky for three nebbishes to attempt without any kind of proper equipment. “Didn’t we have a rope?” Hill asked.

“Left it for the sheep.”

“Crampons, then?”

“We’re not having our periods.” Dell beat Drew to it, and they giggled as Hill rolled ‘moron’ eyes at them. The levity did nothing to alleviate the situation. After a moment more of failing light, Drew said, “I suppose we have to try,” and sidled over to the closest mass of crap rock between the Pillar and Kerwriggle and placed his hands on it, and felt for handholds. He hauled himself up a bit and then back down. “I suppose we could do this,” he said doubtfully.

Dell toned in a British newsman’s voice, “The mystery of the missing Americans was solved today when local goatherds found three broken bodies at the base of Kerwriggle. The idiots actually tried to climb it.” And he looked balefully at Drew, who gave him an ‘alright, alright’ wave. “There’s gotta be a way,” he insisted, then turned to Hill. “Anything in these Elidar or Arthur legends that might give us a clue?”

“Nothing comes to mind, but maybe ...” and he pulled out the scroll and held it up eye level, but there was no blue light this time.

Instead, something moved.

Startled, Drew leaped back from the base because the movement was tracing from about where he had been standing and wound its way up the mountain until it disappeared over a shelf. A smattering of dust and gravel fell around them as it did, and they moved hastily away until that stopped. Cautiously, Drew slid back to his former position, cocked his head and, "What the—" then flattened against the mountain and looked up, and then stood back, shaking his head. "Unbelievable," he said.

"What is it?" Dell and Hill asked at the same time, and stepped forward, craning their necks.

Stairs.

"Yeah, I'd say this is probably the right round lake," Dell observed from the front.

"Shut up," Drew retorted, more for the need to save their breath than reassert himself because, even with stairs, this was hard going. Imagine if they'd had to climb.

"Save your breath," Hill gasped from the middle, and Drew wondered if the scroll let him read minds. If so, what am I thinking now, Professor? That Hill didn't react with some offense disproved the theory.

The stairs were convenient but were obviously constructed for smaller medieval feet. Did they have smaller feet back then? Drew thought so, because people were shorter, so why would they have big feet? They'd look like clowns. Maybe they were. Obviously, these stairs would not accommodate big greave-covered knight's feet, so there's little chance they were followed ... yeah, like the knights followed normal physical laws. Nervously, Drew looked down the stairs.

A flicker at the base of the Pillar.

"Hey, guys," he called, "there's something down there."

Everyone came to a wobbly stop and followed Drew's wobbly point down the stairs.

"I don't see anything," Dell said. Which was understandable; the twilight had gathered at the base, turning it into that abyss you weren't supposed to stare into. Drew wondered if he was seeing things, brought on by the uncertain light and dangerous climb. "Well, it's gone now, but that doesn't mean it wasn't there."

"Coming up the stairs?" Hill asked with appropriate worry in his voice.

"What?" Dell responded, "like another hiker?"

Drew blinked at him. "No, Dell, not a hiker."

They frowned at each other. They frowned at the ground below. Then scrambled up the steps much faster now, practically crawling on all fours. Fortunately, every thirty feet or so, a landing appeared and they caught their collective breath, took another look behind, and launched up the next set.

As stars began shimmering in the twilight sky, Dell pulled up sharp. "I'm at a ledge," he reported. "This must be it."

Hesitation, now, on the verge of whatever had brought them here at Drew's considerable expense, boom or bust or evisceration by dead knights. Dell shrugged, "What the hell," and pulled himself up and over. Hill gave an identical shrug and followed, and Drew waited a moment for their severed heads to be flung back over, but that didn't happen, nor were there screams of terror.

So do this. With a final push off the step, he rolled over the top and right into the legs of the other two, who were standing side by side and facing the mountain. “What?” he asked and then leveraged up until he was next to Dell. And saw what.

A cave. A blue luminescence outlining it. And standing in front of it, ghost knights.

Lots of ghost knights.

“Crap,” he said.

The knights stood in a loose formation, vaguely semicircle, but well within support of each other, anticipating Dell and Drew and Hill would try to rush through them. All their eyes glowed blue, and they held their swords up at helmet level, the blades pointed skyward. Drew looked back down the stairs and wondered how far they could get before the knights overwhelmed them. Maybe about three steps.

Tableau. Three idiots facing off against a platoon of monsters. The time stretched and finally, Drew shuffled a bit. “How come they haven’t killed us yet?”

“I ... don’t know.” Hill was genuinely puzzled.

“Maybe they’re savoring the moment,” Dell offered.

That made sense. “How many are there?”

“I counted twenty-four,” Dell said.

“So, eight each. We can take ’em.” When nobody laughed, Drew said, “I thought there were only six or seven Round Table knights. You know, Galahad and Percival, that lot.”

“Some sources number them up to 1500,” Hill said.

“Mighty big table,” Dell observed.

“So, then, even if we get through these guys, there could be a thousand of them waiting inside,”

Drew concluded. Great.

The nervous conversation among them did nothing to stir the knights. They were still, watching, and after a few more minutes, Drew shook his head impatiently. “Alright, I’m done with this. Some other treasure hunter can find my shredded body in a few years.” And he deliberately stepped forward, shrugging off Dell’s frantic grab at his shoulder and Hill’s gasp. Five steps and he was in front of the lead knight, whose blue glowy eyes shifted as he approached, but the sword remained aloft. Drew stood, daring the knight’s forbearance. “C’mon, tin can, do something,” hc taunted. Nothing.

Drew took a tentative step past the lead knight into the ranks and braced for a rain of Morgul blows, but still nothing. He blinked around him, then took several more steps, until he was in the middle of the squad and the cave lay before him. He turned to the others. “Coming?” he asked and stepped through the last line of knights until he was at the cave mouth. Dell and Hill joined him a few moments later.

“How did you know?” Dell asked.

“I didn’t.”

“*Hmph*,” Dell tsked, “you’re always the one, ayncha?”

Yes, yes he was, and they smirked at each other.

“I don’t think it’ll be as easy leaving,” Hill, who had turned about and eyed the knights, said. Dell and Drew looked back. The knights had not moved, were still facing the stairs.

“So we check in, but we don’t check out,” Dell summed. “Okay.” He flourished arms at the cave.

"After you, Alphonse," he said to Drew.

"Indubitably, my good man, but I insist you precede me, Gaston."

"I could not think of it and must insist that you precede *me*, Alphonse."

"Perish the thought, my boon companion!" Drew placed a dramatic hand across his chest, "It is your true honor to lead the way."

"But then I would rob *you* of that honor—"

"Oh, for God's sake," Hill muttered and pushed past them.

They both watched him go, grinned at each other, linked elbows, and followed.

The blue light faded to just a suggestion the deeper they went, so it was difficult to make out detail. A cave. Rocks. What more do you want?

"We sure about this?" Drew asked.

There was a slow brightening down the way, a yellowish light, candles, or torches or a Balrog—who knew—and it gave them a better line to follow than the blue glow. It didn't help with their footing, and a few times Drew almost pitched over from catching a hidden rock or rise.

"Could you be louder, please?" Dell said. "I don't think Smaug quite knows we're here."

"Smaug, huh? I was thinking Balrog."

"Probably trolls."

"Would you two shut up?" Hill was truly irritated. Evidently, he did not know the tension-relieving effects of silly banter. So they accommodated him.

The yellow light grew steadier from around a

sharp corner, which meant they would step directly into the view of whatever dragon or demon sat there. Drew briefly thought of shoving Hill in front of them so he could be eaten first, but ultimately, that would serve to divide them when they needed the solidarity. "Together," he announced, because he could see that Dell was thinking the same thing, and they, more or less, rounded the turn together.

Not quite what he expected.

No dragons, trolls, demons, or even ghost knights, for one thing. A grotto, the back part of it blue lit in the same shade as the guiding light in concentric circles, rounding from the top of the cave to the floor and then diminishing into a blue distance, which reminded Drew of that old show *The Time Tunnel*. There was a pool at the base of the grotto, blue and tinkling like a crystal, which he realized was due to water dripping from the roof. Torches lined the walls, spaced evenly from the grotto to where they stood. Drew looked at them suspiciously. Who was lighting these?

Probably the guy lying on the altar.

"What. The. Eff?" Dell breathed.

Which was an excellent reaction. The altar was a wonder of gold and lapiz lazuli and pearl and ruby and marble; a brace of tall brass candelabras descended from the side of it down marble steps to the marble floor right before them. A red flag with a golden dragon draped the altar, folded like July 4th bunting.

And on it was a king.

Prone, his hands folded together, replicating those medieval tombs, full silver armour from chest to foot that sparkled in the candlelight, a simple gold crown on a head full of brown curly locks, over a forehead lined with care and worry, eyes closed, mouth a tight line, holding a sword.

The sword.

Despite all the fascinating things to stare at, the sword caught all their attention. Black handled, not gold, which was unexpected but more practical. You certainly don't want to fight with a sword that could be bent where you're holding it. The hilt was a deep copper color and had to be a fairly strong alloy to ward blows, but Drew couldn't guess what. The blade … my goodness. A glowing, bluish metal, like the steel from a meteor, carbon and lightning, with sparks flying up and down it. Eldritch. Fey.

"Oh, my," Hill whispered and stepped forward, hand outstretched, mesmerized.

"Hold on a second, chief," Drew said, grabbing his elbow sleeve.

"Oh, my," Dell whispered and also stepped forward, mesmerized and reaching for the altar.

"Dammit!" Drew muttered and grabbed his sleeve, too, and wondered why he always had to be the adult in the room I mean, guys, yes, it's beautiful, it's so beautiful, and there is so much power in it, the power of gods and time and infinity and it rules nations and worlds and universes if he could just grasp it …

"Wait!"

Drew blinked and stopped his hand only inches from the hilt and looked over at Dell's hand parallel to his and Hill's, who had stepped back, his face white as the ghost knights, then seized both of them and yanked them back with a strength they didn't know he had. "Wait!" he repeated.

"Why?" Drew asked.

"Yes, why?" Dell echoed, and the two of them tried to shake Hill off, but he had them in talon grips.

"Because we are not worthy."

That was so absurd that Drew actually laughed, which broke the spell, and he looked at where he was and what he was about to do, and maybe they should be circumspect about this. Dell, fortunately, reached the same conclusion, and they nodded at each other, and stepped back to a safer distance, Hill guiding them away and not too gently.

"Okay, you can let go now," Drew said with warning in his voice, and Hill did so immediately, and then made a production out of brushing his coat to let Hill know not to grab him again. "What do you mean we're not worthy?"

Hill was breathing deeply, sweat on his forehead, which was telling, given the coolness of the cave. "Only Arthur can wield Excalibur."

"You mean, that guy?" Dell gestured at the king.

"I believe that's him, yes."

"Well," Dell said, somewhat miffed, "he doesn't look like he's doing too much wielding these days, although," Dell scrutinized the body, "he looks pretty good for a thousand-year-old corpse."

"Closer to two thousand."

"Fine. So why can't we touch it, then? He's obviously in no shape."

Hill took in a deep breath. "Because, it's like Thor's Hammer. You have to earn the right."

"And how does one earn such a right?" Drew asked in his best Oxford accent.

"Well, you have to pull it from the Stone."

"What Stone?"

"Precisely," Hill said and took a significant look around the chamber, which was Stoneless. Or, at least, contained nothing that could be so construed.

"Okay, great. So what if we ignore that whole Stone thing, and just assert our rights under 'Finders Keepers'?" Drew asked.

"I think that would be very bad," Hill toned.

"What kind of bad? We get a bad review at work or a pimple right before a date?"

"*Pffht*," Hill razzed, "You'd hope for that. I'm thinking like what happened to those Nazis when they touched the Ark."

They got the reference. All three stared at the sword, so close, beckoning.

"So, what then?" Dell threw his hands up in exasperation. "We take a few photos and load them on Facebook, look what I did for summer vacation?"

"Autumn," Drew corrected.

"Whatever."

"No, no," Hill waved his hand, "we should probably do something. Take a token of some kind."

"Those jewels on the altar look like a decent token," Drew said. And would probably go a long way to relieving his card debt. He fished for his pocket knife.

"I think that would be as bad as touching the sword. No," he looked about helplessly, "we need some kind of token or boon from the Lady of the Lake."

"You mean a watery tart dispensing swords as a means of establishing supreme executive power?" Dell deadpanned.

Hill grinned. "Well, no, even if some moistened

bint threw a scimitar at me," and they all guffawed because they got the reference.

"Wouldn't that be a token?" Drew pointed out.

"No," Dell cut in, "just some farcical aquatic ceremony!"

And here they just lost it, laughing uproariously and slapping each other on the back and falling about the place. It was a wonder the king did not rise up and smite them.

Someone else did.

There was a shuffling behind, and Drew looked and stopped laughing and stood up straight, and the other two did the same, no longer amused.

Three women stood in the turn. No, not women, that was too small a word: goddesses, angels, nereids, fairy queens. A light shimmered about them, a holy light of silvered moon, their golden tresses past their shoulders to their waists drifting as if some mistral caressed them, a golden belt held by an emerald clasp kept their pure white robes closed, but that was just a token to modesty because the bodies underneath were the desire and passion a man would die for.

Drew almost fell to his knees. "My God," he whispered.

"My God," Dell and Hill said.

The three women all smiled at the same time, sunrise over a darkened moor, and their eyes of the same blue as the cave light flashed with benevolence and urge and hither, come hither, and Drew felt his feet obeying.

"No," Hill warned, but it was obvious he was having as hard a time resisting as Drew. Dell had no problem; he'd already gone to his knees, induced to cross the distance on them.

"Are they the Lady of the Lake?" Drew didn't care, at this point, about subject/verb agreement.

"The taller one in the middle probably is," Hill, with proper awe, whispered. "The other two are probably attendant priestesses."

"I would very much like to attend her," Drew decided.

"As would I," Hill nodded, and they would have crossed the distance, except the queens stopped smiling. And the blue of their eyes turned into storms.

"Uh oh," Drew said.

Uh oh, indeed.

A shadow behind them, like smoke, drifted past the three and settled in the distance between them and the boys, a green, oily smoke with red lights running through it, and it swirled and it became a man.

In theory.

"Holy crap," Dell breathed from his now standing position. Which summed up Drew and Hill's reaction.

It was not quite solid, shifting up and down like swamp air, a fell ghost of rot and lost souls. A balding man, the black hair on each side still thick and full but with a wrinkled pate of greenness, the color of disease, decomposition, maggots plying graves, hinged over a great pair of eyebrows as thick as a man's wrist. And the eyes, hooded ... black. No, red. Hell light. A nose like a ship's prow and a mouth of cruelty and hate lording over a pointed beard like Satan's.

And it was not happy to see them.

"What. The. Eff. Do. We. Do?" Drew's terrified whisper to Hill.

"I. Don't. Know." Hill's terrified whisper back.

Great.

They stood transfixed as the thing swayed from side to side, examining them carefully, as if sizing up who to eat first. Then slowly, murderously, it flowed forward and stood right before Hill, its death eyes and mouth mere inches away from the Professor's face.

This is it, Drew thought, this is how I die, cast into hell by one of Satan's chief demons ...

"Merlin." Hill's squeak made the thing smile thinly.

Oh, crap, even worse, a powerful wizard from ancient times mightily torqued at these foolish mortals disturbing his charge, good ole King Arthur asleep at the wheel over there, and having designs on the Sword of Eternity and, well, what will be their fate? Tied to a mountaintop while bats eat our livers for a few thousand years, he supposed.

The thing bore down on Hill then, inexplicably, held out his hand.

"What?" Hill was frantic. "What does he want?"

"A high five?" Dell offered and, well, no.

Merlin shook the hand at Hill, obviously growing angrier, if that was possible.

"I don't know what it wants!" Hill's desperation grew, and Drew was sure Merlin was going to bite off the Professor's head like Ozzy Osbourne contemplating a bat, when he suddenly knew.

"The scroll," he said.

"What?" Hill looked at Drew curiously, breaking contact with Merlin, which meant it needed something else to look at and, of course, that was Drew, and he felt his soul shrivel.

"The scroll! The map! The case! Give it to him!" Before one of those long green talons Merlin had for fingernails plunged into Drew's stomach and pulled out his intestines.

Hill didn't quite comprehend, and Drew braced for evisceration when the Professor said, "Oh," and reached into his coat and pulled out the scroll.

Merlin immediately switched his attention from eating Drew to Hill, his hand out again, and Hill placed the scroll gingerly in it, which closed. And then the other hand came out, insistent.

"What does it want now?" Hill mouthed.

Drew was at a loss.

"The box!" Dell, who hadn't really contributed that much up to this point, said brightly.

Of course. Drew could have kissed him, but didn't want to draw any more unwanted attention. "Give him the box!" he urged.

"I don't have it." Hill was shaking in terror.

"What?" Drew was suddenly too angry to be scared. "What do you mean? You had it this whole time!" That idiot professor's absent-mindedness was going to get them all killed. Killed? Enslaved to trolls.

"It's in my backpack," Hill nodded toward the cave turn. "It's there. Next to the Lady."

So it was. And what good would that do them now, because Merlin was not happy with this conversation. His lizard-thick skin seemed to swell more and there was roiling under his cheekbone, and Drew just knew a set of alien jaws was going to plunge right through Hill's brain, followed by a face hugger just for insult.

"*Ahnsyo*!" or something like that from the front of the cave, in a voice of silver bells and moon harps, and Merlin slowly turned about, and all of them looked where the Lady of the Lake held the box up in triumph, the backpack discarded at her feet. Merlin regarded her for a moment, nodded, and then turned back to Hill.

This is it. Laborers in a diamond mine at the center of the Earth for eternity.

Merlin shifted up and down for a moment, measuring Hill, and then drifted in front of Dell, who braced and turned his face away with a look of utter revulsion, which indicated Merlin's pretty horrid breath, which Drew confirmed when Merlin then chose him for an examination. Oh, God, so that's what Hades smells like. No wonder Satan avoids the place.

The reek followed Merlin as he eased back, still floating over the floor, no feet apparent, just the shredded remains of his grave cloak, and he stopped in front of the Ladies.

"Nice knowing you," Drew said to Hill.

"It has been an adventure," Hill answered.

"I want Mommy," Dell declared, and that was a nice sentiment.

Merlin, suddenly tall and black and terrible, his eyes growing in red and heat and power until it was a sun blasting everything, and Drew shielded his face, but it was too much, too much, and he screamed.

Just once.

Rain.

Drops of cold water and mist plied Drew's face as he wondered what kind of hell was made of water when he opened his eyes to a nice shower merrily spraying drops all over him. Great. Merlin sent us to Seattle. Starbucks hell.

He wiped his face and sat up and blinked about him, but there wasn't much to see, just mist and rain, and he could stand an umbrella. At least it was a comfortable Seattle hell. He looked down and saw, in the very dim light, his backpack. And duffel bag. And the other equipment they'd left at the sheepfold. Which was right in front of him, the streetlight above just bright enough to see. "What the eff?" he asked the rain.

"What the eff?" from Dell, who was sitting next to him. They looked at each other in surprise, sure that chains and manacles had them bound to some ogre's back, but no, they were simply wet.

"I want Mommy?" Drew said.

"Shut up," Dell said and pushed him away.

Drew got his feet underneath him and staggered up and checked himself for dragon bites or some kind of demon tattoo, but nothing. A groan off in the mist identified Hill's location and Drew walked over, almost stepping on the Professor, but reaching down and helping him up.

"Where are we?" Hill asked.

"It's either Seattle or the sheepfold where we started this mess. And look," Drew waved an expansive hand around them. "Our equipment is still here." Good. He could at least get his money back for that.

Hill looked about him, confused. "I don't

understand."

"Neither do I, but I'm not complaining. I think we should thank Merlin and get as far away from here as we can." And he grabbed bags and duffels and started arranging them for a hasty flight.

Dell was standing at the sheepfold, frowning in the general direction of Kerwriggle. "But, it's right over there." A point in that direction.

Drew dropped the bag he was arranging. "Do you seriously want to go through that again? You were calling for Mommy at one point." The point they should have died, except for Merlin's mercy.

"Yeah, but," Dell made a helpless gesture, "all this way and we've got nothing to show for it."

"You have a lovely story you can tell Mommy when we get back home."

"Listen, you," Dell took a threatening step toward him ...

Clink!

Dell leaped back as if he had stepped on a snake, peered down. "What's this?" he said and hefted what, based on the effort, was a heavy leather bag.

"I don't remember buying that," Drew said, and he placed a supporting hand under the bag because it was substantial. Looked like one of those bags from a *Dungeons and Dragons*' game, one of those Bags of Holding ... "No way," he said and pulled it to him with a "Hey, man!" protest from Dell, and undid the leather tie and looked inside and had his breath taken away, and he set the bag down on the ground.

Dell stepped up and looked. "Oh, my."

Hill joined them. "Oh my," he repeated.

Gold coins, jewels, silver, all kinds of treasure glinted at them. Well, looks like he'd pay off his credit cards after all.

"Good enough," Dell said.

"You know," Drew mused, "since this didn't come out so bad, and since we are here ..." He raised his eyebrows, "Loch Ness?"

Hill and Dell looked at him like he was crazy.

But only for a moment.

The Inspiration

I. Vampires

A. Books

1. The classic is, of course, Bram Stoker's *Dracula*, which is still the best novel for vampire lore. Practically every other vampire book borrows from it. Stoker accumulated numerous legends and myths from various traditions to create the vampire we have all come to love. So if there's one in your neighborhood and you need a quick brush-up on how to get rid of it ...

2. *Salem's Lot*, Stephen King. Still the best 'modern' vampire tale because it updates Stoker to this century ... well, close enough. All those other 'modern' vampire novels that follow families and covens and angst-ridden shiny boys, meh.

B. Movies

1. Bela Lugosi's *Dracula* is considered the classic but, man, is it slow. The 1979 Dracula, starring Frank Langella, is a far more faithful adaptation of the Stoker novel, and quite decent.

2. Any Count Yorga movie.

3. More recently, *Let the Right One In* is faithful to the legend, and an overlooked gem is the Iranian movie, *A Girl Walks Home Alone at Night*.

II. Creatures from Lagoons, Black or Otherwise

A. Books

1. Anything by HP Lovecraft.

2. *Jaws*, although it's just nature, man. Not malicious. No, not at all.

B. Movies

1. *Creature from the Black Lagoon*. The classic.

2. *Gorgo*. The American Godzilla.

III. Dr. Jekyll and Mr Hyde.

A. Books

1. The Robert Louis Stevenson classic.
2. *The Picture of Dorian Gray*, Oscar Wilde.

B. Movies

1. The Frederick March classic.
2. And just for fun: *The Daughter of Dr. Jekyll*

IV. Werewolves

A. Books:

1. Like vampires, there's a ton of werewolf books, the classic being *The Werewolf of Paris* by Guy Endore. Stephen King's *The Cycle of the Werewolf* is another good one.
2. Avoid the ones that try to make them all angtsy. Werewolves are monsters, not misunderstood teenagers.

B. Movies

1. Tons of good werewolf movies, starting with Claude Rains' *The Wolf Man*. His way is thorny.
2. Modern werewolf movies have been more true to the character than modern vampire movies, two standouts being *An American Werewolf in London* and The Howling.

V. Frankenstein

A. Books

1. The original, Mary Shelly's *Frankenstein*.
2. Brian Aldiss, *Frankenstein Unbound*, a sci-fi novel about a sci-fi novel.

B. Movies

1. The original Boris Karloff.
2. *The Curse of Frankenstein*, which inspired Wilfred.

VI. Ghosts

A. Books

1. Lots of classic ghost stories out there, mostly as parts of story collections. *Great American Ghost Stories* is one, and any Alfred Hitchcock anthology.

2. Everyone says *The Haunting of Hill House* by Shirley Jackson, but it never moved me. Better ones are *The Shining*, Stephen King, and *Ammie, Come Home* by Barbara Michaels.

B. Movies

1. Lots of classic ghost movies, too, but one of the earliest and still one of the best is *The Uninvited*, *The Terror* and *Cry of the Banshee* are some good 'uns.

2. *The Changeling* is, IMHO, the best modern ghost movie made.

VII. The Mummy

A. Books

1. I have not read that many books with mummies as the center, but Bram Stoker's *The Jewel of the Seven Stars* is probably the prototype, and probably inspired Boris Karloff's The Mummy. Probably.

2. The Goosebumps series has a few dedicated to mummies. Goosebumps is always a fun read.

B. Movies

1. Boris Karloff's *The Mummy*, as previously mentioned.

2. The update with Brendan Fraser is a fairly decent, if a little silly, movie in its own right.

3. As for King Arthur, hands down best movie ever made on the subject: *Excalibur*.

VIII. The Invisible Man

A. Books

1. The original classic, H. G. Wells' *The Invisible Man*. Another classic is Ambrose Bierce's short story *The Damned Thing*, which is an invisible

monster.

2. I have not read any modern novels dedicated exclusively to physical invisibility, so I can't recommend any. Lots of invisibility as plot devices (Cloaks of Invisibility, etc.) but not the subject.

B. Movies

1. Claude Rains again, _The Invisible Man_.

2. Just about every modern treatment of this has been terrible. I can't recommend any of them. Elizabeth Moss's movie, _The Invisible Man_, might be decent, but I haven't seen it.

IX. Zombies

A. Books

1. The classic definition of zombies are the dead brought back to life by a voodoo priest to do their bidding. Probably the best book with this definition is _The Serpent and the Rainbow_, which is also a decent movie.

2. For the George Romero zombie, my goodness, so much to choose from, but Max Brooks. _World War Z_ is a good place to start.

B. Movies

1. For the classic voodoo, _White Zombie_. Bela Lugosi.

2. For the modern re-interpretation, _Night of the Living Dead_. Romero, once more.

These should get you started.

About the Author

D. Krauss was born in Germany, adopted by a military family, and so became a US citizen in a roundabout way. He lived in Oklahoma and Alabama, somehow ending up in New Jersey where he lived every single Bruce Springsteen song. He joined the USAF, staying twenty years longer than intended. He has been a cotton picker, sod buster, painter of roads, surgical orderly, weatherman, librarian, special agent, analyst, and a bus driver. D's been married over 50 years (yep, same woman) and has a wildman bass guitarist for a son. You can reach him at http://www.dustyskull.com.

OTHER BOOKS BY D. KRAUSS

The Frank Vaughn Trilogy:

The Partholon Trilogy:

The Ship Trilogy

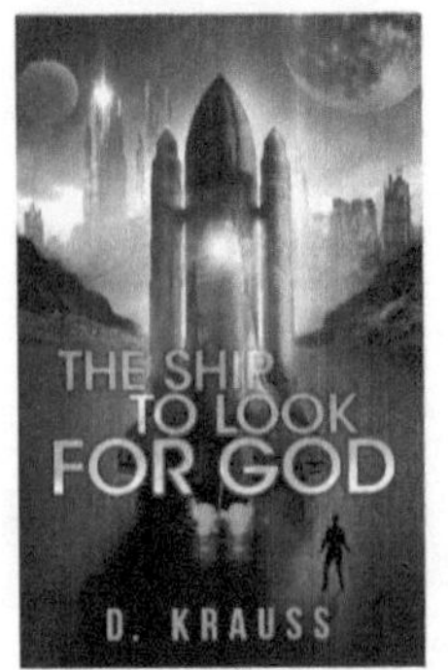

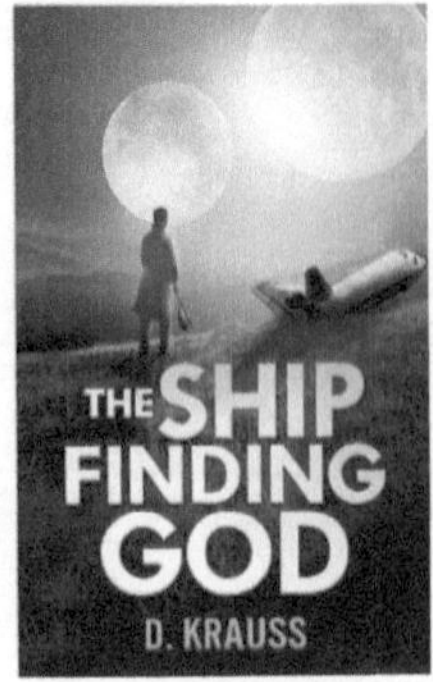

Story Collections

Young Adult

www.indiesunited.net/d-krauss

Cassandra Harris is a Seattle-born illustrator who graduated from North Seattle College with an Associate of Fine Arts (AFA) in arts. She's now based in Houston, where she's thriving her career as an illustrator. She's constantly stumbling into the next interesting book, so you can contact her at:

mae40221@gmail.com

www.ingramcontent.com/pod-product-compliance
Lightning Source LLC
Chambersburg PA
CBHW030519310726
48979CB00010B/1731/J

* 9 7 8 1 6 4 4 5 6 8 8 0 4 *